All is Lost

Stephanie Hunt

Contents

Before

For as long as Elodie could remember, she's been either ignored or stared at with disgust. There was no in between. She didn't stop when she broke out of the palace, she didn't stop when people on the streets stopped to stare, she didn't stop when shouts rang out behind her, and she didn't even stop as her surroundings went from foreign buildings to towering trees.

Even now that it was behind her, she still clutched at her red locks with shame. Rytaria was so much different than what she was used to back on Earth.

That's not the surprising part about it. It's an alien planet, so of course Elodie expected changes and differences. But the differences she did experience upon arrival were not what she was expecting.

She knew her whole miserable life that she was ugly. She was told on a regular basis. It was practically ingrained in her that she would never find a husband, because no man wanted the curse of red haired children dotted in horrific freckles. All along she was aware of her ailment, but still, she held out hope.

Every day she would sneak a romance book out from under her pillow. She would read her favorite lines over and over, dreaming of having love. Longing for a man that would treat her well and adore her as she adored him. But she knew deep down, and with much disappointment, that it wasn't possible for her.

Until now.

Elodie walked down the hallway, looking over her shoulder regularly in case she was being followed. She was.

The massive alien called Locanas was a high ranking warrior. He had many admirers and respect, but not from Elodie. She ducked behind a pillar, determined to hide as she held her breath.

The day she heard of the massive, scary men around their compound on Earth, she had been afraid. Until she realized what it could mean for her. Would these strangers bring her a shot at love? Such a miracle couldn't be possible. Could it?

Turns out, it was, but not in a way she could ever dream. Aliens. The newcomers were aliens. And Elodie found out the hard way.

It was all because of one big burly alien that grabbed her. Locanas. He still terrified her, even now that she was safe and far away from Earth, tucked in an enormous palace where she wanted for nothing. But she still didn't have what she wanted most. Romance.

Now it seemed even more far fetched to desire such a thing. It was clear, even though they couldn't communicate, that he wanted her. Desperately.

The only problem was that he was very demanding and didn't take no as a final answer. In fact, it seemed that he didn't understand the word no at all, even though he was lucky enough to have a translation chip, where she had none.

Stupid alien man.

"Elodie." The rough voice had Elodie jumping so high that one of her shoes almost came off.

She didn't have to look up to see who had called her name. It was Locanas, and she knew it, he always managed to find her somehow. He was like a bloodhound finding his prey. Reluctantly, she looked up at the massive alien.

He was close to 7 feet tall, which was the norm for their race. Some were bigger than Locanas, some were smaller, but they were all incredibly massive. It made Elodie feel insignificant. But to Rytarians, she was anything but that, they were basically worshipped here because

Rytaria had no females. Their race was dying out. They needed human women desperately.

But despite the fact that nearly 50 women came to live on Rytaria from Elodie's community alone, Locanas only wanted her, and she could not understand why.

"Locanas." She acknowledged, trying to keep the trembling from her voice. She wished for her best friend suddenly, Soleil was always the strong one, the brave one. What she lacked in height, she made up for in heart.

The alien male reached out to touch her, and she took a step back. He did not like that. Letting out a growl, he pushed her against the pillar, pressing his hard muscular body against her soft one.

Panicked, Elodie whimpered, but she didn't dare scream, too afraid of what he would do to her in retaliation.

"Meseela relinkas, Elodie." He said gently, his voice the opposite of his harsh hands and strength.

Elodie felt like she couldn't breathe. She was trapped completely, and there was no way she could fend off a Rytarian warrior. They were unbeatable. She was basically a child compared to one of them.

"Please." She murmured, but he didn't back off. There was desperation and pleading in his hard eyes, and he just leaned closer.

Elodie turned her head to the side, her heart pounding in her chest. She was absolutely terrified of him. She was frozen. Trembling. Hysterical. She had no idea how she could get out of this, but there had to be a way.

Locanas's hand stretched up, carefully going to her neck and reaching down for the neck of her shirt. His fingers carefully brushed the fabric that hid her body.

Suddenly, a sound rung out through the hallway, and the warrior flinched, his head coming up for a split second.

It was her chance at escape. Ducking under his arm, Elodie quickly freed herself from him. Caught off guard for a moment, Locanas's mouth parted as she sprinted down the hallway. Always determined, he raced after her, boots thudding against the floor behind her.

Panting already, and not looking back, Elodie didn't stop running.

Chapter 1

Barre

The forest is silent and full of peace. The rain mumbles through the leaves, trailing moisture and calm wherever it falls.

I stand on the front porch of my secluded den, staring out into the dense trees. The sun has just risen, a new day cycle starting once again.

My life of serenity is often repetitive, but I wouldn't have it any other way. This is the life I'd always wanted for myself. Predictable. Steady. Stable.

I sip on my cup of steaming cauldri, stirring the bag of dried leaves as the flavors mix. Taking a deep breath of the forest in, I let it out and set my cup down.

Rytaria is going through many changes right now, and I am far away from the bustle of it. In a way I am thankful, but in a whole other way I am restless and curious in ways I never thought possible.

Shaking it off, I begin to prep for my hunt.

Walking to the back shed, I haul the wooden door open, staring at countless creature pelts, antlers, and weapons. I skim the tools with my eyes, quickly deciding which I will use. I look to the top row of weapons, reaching for my hunting bow. I grip it loosely, twirling the thing in my hand. I carved the bow myself, its thick curve perfect for its purpose.

I always spend my time in the woods trailing game, shooting and trapping them for their skins and their meat. I provide for myself so I don't have to be in the palace market, interacting with other warriors who point and stare and whisper.

On Rytaria, I am a legend. One of the last of my kind, the strongest warrior to walk the planet. I do not enjoy the notoriety. Being a Gladiator was my life for several turns, but that was before I quit. That was before the distraction of fights wore off and our society dedicated themselves to finding the one thing that could save us. Females.

Our planet had a disaster long ago, when I was still a young kit. My own Mama dying in our home, my Pa going insane with loss.

Some sort of sickness attacked our females, killing most of them within a few moon cycles. It ruined many lives as a result. As I grew, I learned of my power and how it could help my society.

Gladiator fights became very popular. It was a way to forget the tragedy, a way to forget for a moment's time. It only lasted 10 turns before the desire for it faded away, the loss of females too much to bear.

But now, many have forgotten the battles, and the ring of power and the gladiators alike. And so, I moved into the forest to build my own den far away from the palace and the city. My Papa lived with me for some time before he too succumbed to his death.

And now, it is only me and Salsh, my only companion. The rasler was a stray in the food market, running around in search of scraps. I scooped him up and took him home with me. I can't say that it isn't nice to have some sort of company. Salsh has also become quite the hunter himself. I take him with me on all my outings.

Throwing a sleeve of arrows over my back, I shut the shed and stomp back to the den. The small cabin on my own private land has provided me with comfort ever since I stopped my fights. It has always been able to put me at ease, until now.

Because the Emporor's Warriors have found what they've been looking for all these turns. Females.

The talk of them has spread far and wide. Every time I visit the market I am bombarded by the gossip of males desperate to have a mate of their own. Of course the idea is ridiculous. The first females will go to the elite in the palace, it is obvious. Those of us who do not live luxuriously will be the last to receive a female, if at all. I doubt I will ever get the opportunity, but I do not care.

I am happy to be alone. I do not need anyone else but myself.

I climb the wooden stairs to my porch, leaning down to untie my pet. He sniffs and licks at my side, wagging his tail in excitement. I pat the top of his head in encouragement.

As soon as his leash is off, he sprints into the woods, running circles around the trees, brown fur flying.

Shaking my head in amusement, I follow him. He blazes the trail with his nose to guide him. He leads me through the dense forest, jumping over puddles of rain and ducking under fallen trees.

Taking a deep breath of the fresh air, I let it linger in my lungs, savoring my favorite pastime.

I don't know why, but something tells me today will be different, and maybe in a good way. I find it an odd feeling. Maybe it means I will get a large Lilarc, or many Sylvarons.

I suppose I will just have to find out, and I am very excited for it.

Chapter 2

Elodie

I'm panting with effort, tears streaming down my face as I run. My legs ache from the effort. My heart thunders in my chest like a warning alarm.

I don't know how long I run, but I can't stop. Fear pushes me forward until I'm tripping over rocks and sticks and foliage.

A trickle of rain sleets from above, soaking my hair and pasting my clothes to my skin. The massive sun in the sky begins to rise, casting the forest pink and orange. It was night when I left. I must have been running for hours.

Stumbling, my knees hit a stream of water, I try to catch my breath for only a moment before I shove my hands in the freezing water. I stand as I whip my head around. My eyes search relentlessly through the trees.

Terror sparks as the image of Locanas floats into my mind.

My throat tightens, and I'm afraid I'll throw up.

My wild red hair flies around me as I torpedo through the woods. The cursed color of my locks combined with the brown speckles across my body have been the bain of my existence. My coloring is only a reminder of my pain as a whole new pain comes on.

I can remember every comment, every snide remark, every joke. My Dad's embarrassment and disappointment. He didn't even care when I decided to abandon Earth, all he worried about was his wives leaving him. I was the last thing on his mind.

Tugging free of a low tree branch, I scrape my arm against the bark, ripping open my flesh. I hiss in a panicked flash of pain, the sting dulled out by my adrenaline.

I had thought this new planet would be a new start. It was, but it's not what I thought it would be. I didn't plan on almost getting assaulted by a giant. I thought they worshiped females, we are supposed to be sacred or whatever, but of course I would be the one they see as damaged goods. I'm still less than.

I clutch my red hair as I continue on, tears springing to my eyes at the realization. Maybe red hair is seen as ugly here too. I have yet to see a Rytarian warrior with orange locks. Maybe I'm a curse anywhere I go.

Sniffling, I push a hand into the river, shoving off of a rock and into the woods.

I have no idea where I'm going, or what I'm going to do, I just had to get away. There was so much fear and pressure and unknowns.

All I've ever wanted was romance and love, but now that I finally had a chance at finding someone it got ruined.

It's almost as if Locanas had some sort of claim on me. Other males never came near me, and when he was around they wouldn't even look at me.

Sniffling, I clutch at my injured arm, I make myself move forward. Locanas is so much bigger than, and much bigger. That means he's faster than me too. The thought shoots a panic through me. I keep going anyway.

I should have known that this planet would be a bust. I'm just not lucky. Maybe I'm not meant to find love. I hate the idea. I've always dreamt of romance. Even if it's hard, I have to face the thought that I might never experience it.

Tears and rain mix on my face to become one, and soon I can hardly see. I pant for air. I force my legs to go as fast as they can. My muscles burn from exertion, on the brink of collapse.

I see something that doesn't blend in with the forest. It's a sign I realize. A wooden sign nailed to a tree. There's words painted in black, words in a language I can't even begin to understand.

My heart thuds heavily in my chest. I don't know what it says, I have no idea what I'm getting into, but whatever it is must be better than what's behind me.

So, taking a chance, I keep going. My steps become sloppy. The rain falls harder. My blood thunders through my ears, making it impossible to hear.

My arm throbs, but I ignore it. Surely there must be someone out here, there was a sign after all.

Tree after tree passes me by, and nothing looks safe. It's all endless. Nothing but endless woods and rain and pain.

I trip, an unexpected stumble that has me smacking into the ground. I yell out in pain, my ankle twisting in a way it's not supposed to.

But I can't stop, I won't. I have to keep going. I try to get back up, but my legs crumples, no strength left in them. A rips free of my throat as I desperately try to stand.

It's no use. I'm trapped on the forest floor until my strength returns.

Next I decide to hide. I'm small. Surely that will give me some advantage on the monstrous alien man.

I stare around the forest with a new sight. Even the trees here are bigger. They tower high above me, covered in dark bark and like green moss. A light drizzle of rain is constantly going. No wonder the trees are enormous, they're always being watered.

I start crawling to the nearest tree, clawing the damp soil, grabbing thick roots that peek out from the ground.

The one if pick for sanctuary has a little alcove hidden at the base of the trunk. I curl up inside it, and it gives me a bit of shelter from the constant rain. I close my eyes, trying to pretend like none of this is real.

I picture the endless green fields in Tennessee. My home. The flowers. The river. The hot sun and the humidity. I shiver in the darkness, and a summer's day seems so far away.

My ankle throbs, my arm bleeds, my eyes leak. Allowing myself to cry is a blessing. Sobs rip free, my desire to stay hidden and quiet is gone. I just want to be sad.

Eventually the crying subsides. I lay still against the tree, sniffling and shivering. I keep my eyes closed tight. The only sound I hear is the rain. The forest. It's all that exists.

That is until I hear sniffing. And it's not coming from me. My eyes fly open as my heart rate triples in speed.

I'm met with a big, black nose. Red eyes. Horns.

It's a... dog. Or something close to a dog.

The dog like creature raises its ears. He's enormous. Bigger than any dog I've seen or heard of. He gets closer, shoving his face in the tree hole, sniffing at my tear soaked cheeks.

He licks at the salty rivers, and I giggle despite the situation. He sniffs everything on me. My ears, my nose, my mouth, making a gruff purr in his throat.

Of everything I expected, this definitely wasn't part of it. A feeling of safety washes over me. I stiffen. Someone is outside. Close by.

Oh crap.

Chapter 3

Barre

When Salsh lifts his snout to the wind, I know that he's discovered something. The rain slices down around us, but he's still able to uncover scents lying underneath the wetness.

"Go." I order a one word command that he knows well. He pads through the underbrush in a hurry, leading me to the prey.

I sling the bow off my back, pulling a long arrow out of my pack and loading the string. The coarse feathers tickle my fingers as I move forward in anticipation.

I'm on guard, moving slowly and quietly to not scare off my victim. One glance and a Lilarc would run the other way. They are skiddish creatures. I have to be careful.

I look ahead, seeing that Salsh has stopped in front of something. I spot a small flash of movement, the scent of blood wafting to me, and I pull my weapon up to my face as I take aim. I must be quick.

Whatever it is, it's injured and cannot run. My rasler has it cornered, huddled inside a tree pathetically awaiting its death. I will give it what it wants.

I squint, holding my arrow at the ready, seconds alway from shooting, and that's when the little thing moves. Long, red strands of hair come into view. I pause. My weapon remains firmly in my grasp.

What have I discovered?

I have never seen a creature with red fur.

Curiosity gets the best of me, so I lower my bow and arrow, slinging the thing over my shoulder once again as I make my way to whatever this thing is.

The first thing I notice is that Salsh is wagging his tail in excitement, which is rare. When I step into the scene, I look past my pet to discover something I never expected. A female.

My steps falter. I stand as still as stone, my muscles tightening in alarm as I drink in the sight of the tiny she.

She's huddled inside the base of a tree, her clothing wet and sticking to her trembling frame. She clutches at her body, rolled into a tight ball of shivering limbs. I can barely see her.

When she spots me, she whimpers.

Her sad green eyes are filled with tears, and she stares at me with so much fear that I might choke. Her hair is dampened by the rain, but I can see the strange color of it from here. And her pale face is speckled with brown flecks. She must be covered in dirt.

I cannot believe that this is happening. I knew the capitol had females, but why is there one here? On my lands? Injured and alone?

My chest constricts at seeing such a beautiful, helpless creature. She is so small. I remember when female Rytarians walked the planet. They did not look like this tiny thing before me. But she is not Rytarian. She is a "human".

I feel my throat burn, my heart thudding erratically. She does not look away from me.

"Are you... are you alright?" I murmur, too afraid to get close out of fear of frightening her off. She needs medical care. I stare vehemently at the tear on her forearm, red blood pouring out. Her blood is red. How odd. Red hair and red blood. Unheard of.

She doesn't respond, and I wonder if she has no translation device. I do not have one either.

They are not necessary in the woods, and they would break often when I was a gladiator. I have no way of communicating with this perfect being.

And she is perfect. So feminine that I cannot think straight. All I want to do is take her away and care for her. Looking around the forest that is still being covered in rain, I see no male in sight. Somehow, she ended up all the way out here. We are far from the palace, but she got here on her own it would seem.

No male would leave a female in the wood alone. But she has made it this far alive.

So she is not completely helpless, which confuses me. Her soft, small body tells me that she is weak, made for protecting. She is not unscathed from the forest. Her arm wound could be one of many.

It is a miracle I have found her now.

"Do not be afraid." I know there is a possibility that she cannot understand my words, but I must try to soothe her.

Coming closer, I lower myself onto on knee, staring at her as if she will disintegrate.

The female blinks at me, huddling closer to the tree. Salsh follows her movements, nuzzling her face with his nose. He sniffs her hair and her neck.

Amazingly, the female reaches out her hand, tentatively petting the hunting rasler as if she knows him.

And he lets her, happily, a smooth chuff of pleasure leaves his throat.

My mouth parts. Salsh has never let someone other than me pet him. He typically growls and snaps at any hands that reaches for him, but not her. It's as if he knows her priceless value.

"gewd dawgy" She whispers, and then sniffles, tears still leaking down her pink cheeks that look soft to the touch.

Her language is light and airy, her voice the most beautiful sound to have graced my ears.

I gulp, not knowing what to do with myself. Clearly she is afraid. The last thing I want is to scare her even more.

For many I am a hideous beast. I terrify most Rytarians. My name is infamous, my power god like, my scars a curse from my evil occupation. I have never cared how I appear. But now? Now I do.

Does she see what everyone else does?

I shake off the question, moving closer to her. Those dull, green eyes flick back to me, distrust heavy in her gaze. I press my lips together.

"I will care for you. Please. Let me take you away from here." I keep my tone even and soft, and my theory is confirmed when she squints at me, no recognition. She has no translation chip.

Sighing, I put my hand on Salsh's back, giving him a firm pat. If it weren't for him, I may have never found this female.

She would've died out here on her own. The thought drives me mad.

I reach for her slowly, and she doesn't scoot away. I count that as a small success. I touch her pale wrist, lifting it until I can see the scratch.

The wound is spotted with dirt already, the angry skin smothered in red. It leaks continuously, much like her eyes.

"I need to treat this. And soon." I say, more to myself than her. I dare a glance at the female. The fear has evaporated completely. I gasp.

She's... smiling at me.

Her full, pink lips are turning up at the corners, green eyes glinting. I've never seen anything as spectacular in all my cycles.

Clearing my throat, I stand, making a motion for her to follow. She stays sitting in the tree. I rub at my forehead, wondering how I can even begin to get her to follow me.

"You do not want to come with me?" I wonder, but suddenly she's moving.

She crawls out, sitting at my feet with her head turned up to me.

Her legs try and fail to work as she attempts standing. The female makes a sound of frustration, clawing at the tree with effort.

Dear gods. She's too weak to even stand. She looks like a lilarc kit stumbling for footing.

She collapses, and my panic sends me to her side, she falls into my arms, and the feel of her skin against mine is indescribable.

The creature is unbelievably tiny. She must weigh less than Salsh.

"sarryy. iam soe sarryyy" She mumbles, trying to wiggle away, but I don't let her.

She needs shelter, and I'm a fool for letting her stay in the cold for so long. I haul her into my arms, resting her legs over one arm and supporting her back with the other.

The female gasps when I stand, so I freeze. Her dainty arms are wrapped around my neck, her breath tingling my skin with every exhale.

She's so close, pressed against me. Her body is shivering, her soft skin cold to the touch.

I curse myself for allowing her to sit on the ground while I just stared at her.

She deserves better. She's had better, I know simply by the clothes she wears. A dress made of the finest silk, a ribbon in her hair. Even if I didn't know the palace had females, I would take one look at her and know where she came from.

And now I'm going to bring her to my cabin in the woods. It is as far from luxury as a den could get. But now isn't the time for thoughts like that.

She needs a roof over her head, a bed to lay in, warm food in her belly. My den may not be much, but I have the necessities.

There's no more time to waste.

Chapter 4

Elodie

I try to settle, but my spine continues to shake from the cold and the anxiety that have terrorized me today. The fears of Locanas coming after me still plague my thoughts. Every sound, every unexpected movement has me jumping.

But... I'm a bit distracted from all the horror.

An enormous, gorgeous alien has taken me to his home. Atleast, I assume it's his home.

And when I say he's enormous, I mean he is huge. He's the biggest Rytarian I've seen. He's gotta be at least 7'5" or something. And he's a striking contrast to what I'm used to. He was so tender, so calm. I felt safe when he touched me, like nothing bad could ever happen again. It's ridiculous.

He snatched me right out of the woods. He found me with a bow slung over his wide shoulders and an angry expression painted on his face. He looked like an avenging angel, or a Greek god sent to rescue me.

I watch everything carefully now. This cabin was built for him, I'm sure of it. Tall ceilings and giant furniture to match, I feel like a child sitting on his gargantuan couch.

Peeking through the doorway, I spy on him. He moves around the kitchen carefully, not making much noise as the smell of food wafts through the air.

I pull the blanket he draped over me closer as I shiver, daring a glance out the window. The glass is foggy with rain. There are so many shadows and dark spaces where Locanas could be hiding. Growing uneasy, I lean away from the window and focus my attentions elsewhere.

Audomatically I stand, testing my uneasy legs and hurt ankle. I'm feeling much better already. The strength is returning. Hobbling past the roaring fireplace with my busted ankle slowing me down, I make my way into the kitchen. The room is spacious but cozy, continuing the log cabin theme that I've noticed. Everything is made of wood.

I watch the alien man cautiously. He stands over a stove, mixing something in a big black pot. I almost choke when I realize that he's completely shirtless.

His massive back is tan, and dotted in countless scars and angry marks that cover maps of enormous muscle.

Glancing over, I see that he discarded his shirt on the counter tops.

I also realize that the wooden kitchen counter is so high it sits at my armpits. Again, clearly built for a massively tall person, which is not me. I cap out at 5'6". Not exactly anything to brag about, especially around this dude.

The Rytarian male still hasn't spotted me, so I clear my throat.

He turns, eyeing me with furrowed brows. It gives me a chance to get a better look at him, I hadn't noticed him much earlier when I was trembling in his arms.

His dark hair is unkempt, but in an overtly sexy way. There are also hairs all along his jaw, a sprinkling of long stubble that makes him appear rugged.

His eyes are mismatched. One is a warm, electric brown, and the other a calming dark blue. They both glow like stars.

And then there's his scars that continue on his face. They don't detract from his appearance in any way. They don't stand out, you can't even see them unless you look for them. They're faint lines splattered across his skin that hint at stories of his past.

He has a strong nose, and angular cheekbones, and an exquisite jawline.

And then there's his 8 pack. The dude is shredded.

In other words, this stranger is drop dead gorgeous.

"Mashaleeta delet ras Relinkas." He murmurs, his voice so deep and full of gravel I can feel my eyebrows lift. There's something very calming about him.

He points to the living room, and I shrug. Then I see that he's staring at my ankle. He knows I'm hurt.

"I just wanted to see what you were doing." I murmur, and he narrows his eyes at me.

Wait a minute, can he not understand me?

I point to my ear, and then my mouth. His eyes dawn in understanding, and he shakes his head.

Great. This is completely hopeless then. Neither of us understands a single word the other says. This should be interesting.

The warrior man drops his wooden spoon with a sigh and a shake of his head, stomping over to me. My natural reaction is to take a few steps backwards, images of Locanas towering over me flitting into my brain from my memories.

He stops, looking down at me with a gentle look. It's oddly comforting.

Carefully, he places his enormous hand onto my shoulder, his fingers warm and strong. Worry spreads through me, but he doesn't get in my face like Locanas did. He doesn't stare at me in an unnerving way. He just leads me to the living room.

I walk ahead of him, both his hands steering me gently. I stumble once, my stupid sprain driving me crazy.

He stops, and I glance at him in question. He points to the couch with a steely expression that tells me not to question his command.

I nod, hiding my smile as I sit back on the big, cushy couch.

I watch him silently as he bends by the fire, tending to the flames by adding some dry brown brush to it. It ignites, growing and thriving under his care.

It's fascinating, watching a beast of a man being so careful with his large hands.

Something else very interesting is his back and shoulders, bared to my view. The muscles ripple and flex with every simple movement. I put a hand to my mouth, half expecting there to be drool dripping from my lips.

When he turns, I look away, pretending to look around the room instead. It's ridiculously cozy. A huge crackling fire, comfortable furniture and wooden logs for walls. I notice that there are a lot of animal hides laying around. Some look like sheep pelts, super fuzzy and soft.

I would guess he's an avid hunter. The arrows her carried looked deadly. And so did his weird looking dog who is tied up outside.

He must be a successful hunter too. I doubt anything could get away unharmed when he had it in his mind to kill it. But he lives in this place. A quiet, comfortable cabin.

I could get used to this. Not that the palace isn't nice, but the expensive jewels and lavish drapes aren't exactly my style. They're overwhelming and cold. But this place, it's so warm, so inviting.

Mysterious alien guy stands, walking towards me slowly like I might bolt. I stay still, waiting to see what he'll do. He stalks past the couch to a large chest in the corner, which he opens. He digs through it, grabbing something from inside after some rummaging.

He comes back around the couch, and watches me with those warm, mismatched eyes. His face is fierce, but his energy is calm. He holds a small, metallic box in his arms. I clutch my blanket closer.

I assume that he's asking permission to come closer, so I simply nod my head. I was right. He comes forward, kneeling on one knee in front of me. He puts the box on the couch cushion beside me, opening it to display what I can only assume is medical supplies by the looks of it.

"Are you going to patch me up?" I joke, and his lips twitch in amusement.

His huge fingers are careful as they pick through the supplies.

"Rasnaser, fevb alsha res to." His language is so beautiful and strange at the same time. I gulp, nodding as if I understood, which I definitely do not.

He reaches for me, and I pull the blanket away and reveal my injured arm. He raises an eyebrow as he holds out a massive hand. I give him my arm, crusted with blood and dirt. I suppose it's more urgent than a twisted ankle since the cut can get infected, but it definitely doesn't hurt as much.

I can't help but compare our flesh as he turns my limb in his grip. My arms are skinny and dotted with freckles and light red peach fuzz . His arms are roped with thick muscles and covered in tan skin.

The size difference between our bodies makes me nervous, so I glance at his face instead.

The warrior is concentrated, carefully holding my wrist as he examines the deep gouge near my elbow. His fingers are warm and gentle, the skin rough with callouses.

His dark brows furrow, his full lips pursing. I admire his beauty while he takes care of me. He cleans the wound with steady movements. Cleaning the cut stings a little, but I hold very still.

The giant covers my wound with a bandage, keeping it in place by wrapping some kind of gauze around my arm. I flex under his touch, not wanting to be seen as some weak little lamb.

He reaches for my other arm, and I allow it. He turns my limb over, basically assessing me for any more wounds.

"I'm fine, really. That's the extent of my cuts, I promise." I explain, knowing full well he can't even understand me, but trying to communicate with him anyway.

His gaze shoots to my face, and my skin burns with a flush. His eyes simmer, and then his hand reaches for my cheeks. I shy away slightly, but I let him touch my face anyway. I don't really know why, but I trust this guy.

Something about him seems trustworthy, and I can't put my finger on it. When I was around Locanas, I had a pit in my stomach. But with this guy, it just feels right.

"Uhm, okay..." I say as his fingers explore my flushed face. I guess he's never seen someone blush before, and mine is pretty intense.

"I suppose I should introduce myself." I say, grabbing his arm and pulling it away from my cheek.

Holding his wrist in my hand, I notice that I can't even wrap my whole hand around it. Not even close. Thick veins flex under his skin, and then he relaxes, letting his hand fall into my lap when I still hold tightly to him. His arm is heavy, not surprising.

"I'm Elodie." I soon realize that an introduction like that won't work with him, because he stares at me blankly.

As far as he's concerned, my name is just another weird word in the English language.

So, I lift his heavy arm as best I can, and he complies, lifting it with me to ease the burden. I take his enormous hand and splay it across my upper chest, the tips of his fingers brushing my collarbones.

"Elodie. Elodie." I repeat, pointing at myself with my free hand. "Elodie."

Understanding dawns in his gaze, and he nods once.

"Ell-oh-dee." He sounds out in his deep voice, gesturing to me, and I grin in triumph. He gets it!

"Yes. Elodie."

He pulls his hand away from me, and I sigh in longing, suddenly missing the warmth. I don't have to miss it for long, because he grabs my hand, pulling it without difficulty up to his naked chest. I swallow, trying not to enjoy the sensation of rock hard muscles that tempt me from beneath my skin.

"Barre." He grunts, and I squint at him.

Barre? He's named after a bear? Probably not, but it isn't a terrible coincidence. He sort of resembles a bear.

He watches me expectantly, and I grin.

"Barre." I manage, and he nods in approval, amusement shimmering on his face.

Well, I suppose that wasn't the worst introduction in the world. He's definitely intelligent. Maybe it won't be too difficult to communicate with each other after all.

I just hope that my trust isn't misplaced in Barre's hands, because I cannot handle another Locanas.

Chapter 5

Barre

Elodie. A name to go with her beautiful face.

I dig through my medical supplies, pushing aside bandages and ointments. I never use this safety kit since I am rarely injured, but I am glad that I have it now.

The female, Elodie, isn't severely hurt, for which I'm thankful. After taking care of her first injury, I need to address the next one. Her ankle.

I hadn't noticed the sprain until she came into my kitchen, blanket held tightly to her neck as if it would somehow protect her. She kept her weight off her right leg completely, favoring her left.

My eyes are trained to look for weakness or injuries. Being a gladiator and a hunter, this skill has allowed me to seek out my prey's weak spot to make a quick and easy kill.

Now I'm using this skill for the complete opposite. I'm using it for healing, for protecting. It's... strange.

I make eye contact with Elodie, and her eyes are calm. I silently ask for permission as I motion to her hurt leg. She nods her head, pulling away her blanket and the skirt of her dress.

I gulp as she exposes her pale legs to me. She's making herself vulnerable to me, trusting that I will not take advantage.

Lifting her calf, I examine the injury. I notice the brown flecks decorating her skin continue all the way down to her little toes. They are all over her body. I've discovered that they're not pieces of dirt, but it's just how she looks. There's nothing wrong with them.

It's very odd, but fascinating. They're beautiful. She's beautiful.

Her ankle is swollen and angry, the bones feel delicate under my fingers. Her foot is so tiny in my hand, but the shape is no different than my own. Five toes, toenails, and a heel. But she is also different in many ways.

I grab an elastic bandage, placing her foot gently on my shoulder to keep it in place as I wrap her injury. Setting her ankle takes no time at all, but I find myself drawing it out. I want an excuse to be touching for as long as I can.

She has no clue, no idea how tempting she is to me. She stumbled into my lands. She practically fell into my lap. Most males would see her as a gift, a reward, ripe for the plucking. Many would try to lure her into becoming their mate. Elodie is vulnerable and trusting. I could easily take advantage of her.

But I will not.

I may not be as worthy as a palace warrior, but I have honor. Just because I am a heathen, a gladiator, a killer, that doesn't make me a monster.

And not to mention that I am completely undeserving of something as sweet as Elodie. I should not even be touching someone so precious, even to mend her wounds. My hands are dirty, my past muddy, but I still find myself wanting. And oh, how I want her.

Once her ankle is sufficiently wrapped, I let her foot slide down my chest. I stare into her green eyes. Even under her smile, I detect her fear. She was afraid in those woods, trembling when I touched her, jumping at little noises.

Something, or someone, scared her. She was crying. She was hurt. The thought makes me tense with anger.

Elodie makes a mewl, taking her foot out of my lap and leaning away from me. She sees my fury, feels the rage that is surely leaking off of me in waves. The female has no idea that my deadly demeanor is not directed at her.

And I have no way of telling her.

Instead, I try to calm down. I hate seeing her afraid, especially when it's me that she's afraid of.

"I would never hurt you." I vow fiercely, trying to keep my voice soft despite my inner turmoil.

I've hurt many. Killed many. But I would rather hack my own arm off than raise a hand to Elodie.

She shifts in discomfort, pulling at her dress. Her orange eyebrows furrow, creating a small crease between them. It's adorable.

The smell of food becomes stronger around us, and I know its time that she ate something. I straighten, getting closer to the female who is curled up into a ball, her legs to her chest and her chin resting on her knee.

I open my arms to her, halfway on the couch and so close to her that we're almost touching.

"Come, you must get something in your stomach to help you heal." I tell her, and she sniffles slightly, watching me very carefully.

Even if she can't understand me, she's smart. She observes and decides. Elodie is very intelligent, and I will never underestimate her mind.

She crawls forward slowly, my arms still open to her. I reach for her. She doesn't object. In fact, she puts her hands on my shoulders to steady herself. I pick her up, careful to avoid touching her ankle and her arm. I try very hard not to love the feeling of holding her. I have been starved of any physical contact.

I carry her to the kitchen and to the table. I transfer her to one arm, holding her to my chest as I pull a chair out. I place her in the seat gently, not able to help myself when I touch her red hair.

The color is not natural to my own species, and I find myself admiring her uniqueness.

Elodie tips her head back, my hand resting on mer scalp. She once again blesses me with a smile. I give her a small smile that I don't feel. I like her too much, want her too bad.

What is wrong with me?

I turn, releasing her head from my hold and stalking over to the dinner I've prepared for her. I used several vegetables from my garden, and large pieces of lilarc meat. Plenty of seasonings and a rich broth. It's the perfect meal for Elodie to get better.

The sooner she gets better, the sooner I can return her.

I place a large, full bowl of stew in front of Elodie, she looks up at me with a grateful look.

"thaanck yeew" She says, picking up the spoon and looking at the stew curiously.

Clearing my throat, I go back to the stove to pour myself some food. I take a bite to test it as I stand in the kitchen. It does not taste amazing, but it will help her heal. I'm sure it is nothing in comparison to the feasts they have at the palace.

I come back to the table, and I can't help but notice how small this female really is. Her feet do not even touch the floor when she sits in one of my chairs. She's the size of a kit. I would think she is a kit if it weren't for the fact that she has large teats. I try not to look at them, but it's a sure sign of her sex.

I find myself wondering if she's small for her kind, or if all the human females are little.

Pulling my own chair out, I sit down across from Elodie. She eats small bites of the stew, staring at a chunk of meat with reluctance before putting it in her mouth.

She seems to be doing better. I cleaned her wound and set her ankle, but she'll still be limping for awhile, something that worries me to no end. But her tears have dried, her terror easing as she settles in. Elodie appears to be comfortable in my den, something I didn't expect to happen.

She's female. She must be used to being pampered. But she seems content here anyway.

It makes me almost satisfied. To see her eating, warm and safe, and knowing I provided that for her, it pleases me.

The sun is setting, and the rain storm continues to persist outside. The wind rattles a tree against the walls outside. The sound causes Elodie to jump. I automatically reach a hand out, trying to calm her.

"It is alright, you're safe here. I won't let anything hurt you." I promise, and she glances at me. Her frizzy, orange hair is almost completely dry now. Her breathing is uneven and panicked.

Looking at her now, I know my promise to be true. I've never felt so fiercely protective of anything in my life. The feeling is confusing. I should not feel this way, it's dangerous. I enjoy having her here. But I know that she cannot stay here. I can't keep her. Elodie belongs in the palace.

Females are sacred. They deserve to be taken care of, to be spoiled and worshipped. She doesn't belong here. As soon as I'm able, I'll have to bring her back.

But for now, I must take care of her with what I have.

After a few short moments, she calms. Settling back into her chair, she takes a deep breath, picking up her spoon again and staring down at the bowl with pursed lips. I hardly touch my food. I'm too focused on this female that has changed everything with her appearance.

I sip on my stew, trying to distract myself from her.

But suddenly, a crack of thunder shakes the den, rumbling through my chest.

Elodie shrieks. Spilling stew across the table in a whirl of motion. She's standing, looking around wildly, tears already streaming down her face.

I go to her, putting my hands on her shoulder as I go to kneel in front of her, still taller than her even on my knees.

She snaps out of it, looking up at me with a shocked expression. Elodie knocks the breath out of me when she throws herself in my arms, her arms going around my neck as she sobs. My skin becomes wet from her tears. My heart aches.

When my arms go around her in return, I can't bury the feeling that this is right. This is how things are supposed to be. Her in my arms, pressed against my body, her only comfort and protection from the world.

But it won't always be this way. It's temporary.

"Come here, lets get you in your nest. You need sleep, little one." I hush her, picking her up around her back, her legs wrapping around my waist.

I carry her through the kitchen and to my spare room. It's where my Pa used to sleep, but I've kept the nest clean and the blankets fresh. It seemed to be for nothing, but now I know it was for a reason.

Elodie continues to sniffle, clutching at me tightly. I pull the covers back, lowering myself to sit as I attempt transferring her to the nest so she can sleep.

I soon realize that she won't let go. I could easily force her, my strength substantially greater than hers, but I won't. She's trembling, crying, she needs me.

And so, I will be here to comfort her as long as she needs. I hush her, rubbing a hand up and down her delicate spine.

"It will all be alright, little female. You are safe. I will always protect you." I restate, even if she has no clue what I say. It feels good to assure her that I am here.

Time passes, and her tears subside, her body goes still, breath evening. Elodie has fallen asleep in my arms. I stay still for a while longer, just holding her in my lap as the rain comes down noisily outside.

I touch her hair. She's so warm. So perfect. I find it hard to picture my monotonous life before her.

Eventually I have to leave her, so I sigh and shift my hold on the female, slipping her effortlessly into the nest. She sighs, reaching around for me before latching onto a pillow instead. I chuckle quietly as I watch her.

Her face is soft, cheeks round and covered in pink. Her whole being dotted in those brown flecks. She has a small, pert nose with a bump in the middle of the bridge. Her eyelashes are light orange, her eyebrows a darker auburn. Her lips. They're perfect and red and full.

An unfamiliar feeling rises in me, and I have to look away. I better leave her before I convince myself to stay.

So, I sneak out of the room, but not before pressing a secret kiss of desire on her forehead and whispering goodnight.

Chapter 6

Elodie

I'm jolted awake from a bad dream that I don't even remember, gasping for air and sweating from stress. I pant, desperate to get oxygen into my burning lungs.

It's dark. I can hardly see anything, only the blue moon from a window adjacent to the bed.

I glance around uneasily, half forgetting where I am. In a flash of lightening outside, I remember the giant that is Barre. I recall everything he did for me. He rescued me from the woods. Fed me. Fixed up my injuries. Gave me a warm bed to sleep in.

But he's not in the bed beside me, and that's what unsettles me. I wish he was with me. He makes me feel so safe.

I squint out the window, pulling the covers up to my chin as I eye the outside. I think of Locanas. He never gives up, never stops pursuing me. What would stop him now? He's probably out there still, leaving no rock unturned as he hunts me down. He could find me eventually.

The thought of him makes my stomach turn over. I feel nauseated. My heart thumps uneasily in my chest.

I want Barre. Really want him. He's everything I've ever wanted. A sweet, handsome man to take care of me, make me happy. But now I feel reluctant to pursue what I want. What if he thinks I'm ugly? What if he doesn't feel the same way? What if I just end up bothering him?

They're all questions screaming at me from the back of my mind. But right now, I just want him to hold me and help me chase the nightmares away. If I keep thinking about how I wish he was my mate, I'll go crazy.

I want to go to him now.

But, I second guess myself. I don't want to annoy him. He's sleeping. Barre has done so much for me already, he might not take kindly to me sneaking into his room and crawling into his arms.

I'll just have to tough it out. I'll be okay. At least, that's what I tell myself.

I lay still on my side, fluffing my pillow as I try to get comfortable enough to go back to sleep. I clutch the sheets in my fingers as rain somehow still comes down outside.

It rains a lot here, and I used to find the sound comforting. Then I thought about how the sounds could cover up someone outside trying to get in. He could be right outside the window for all I know.

Swallowing the lump in my throat, I look through the glass at the shadows of the forest. Something moves, and I close my eyes tight, trying not to sob as fear pinches every part of me.

My chin trembles as I hold everything in. The dark is terrifying, but I'm too scared to get up and search for a light switch.

What if Locanas sees me? What if he barges in and takes me away? Would Barre do anything about it? Would he let me go thinking I was safe with any Rytarian because they have "honor".

A tear slips down my cheek, and I'm quick to wipe it away. I don't want to be taken away from here. I don't want to go back to the palace, ever.

I miss Soleil, but I was so unhappy there. I was constantly looking over my shoulder, always hiding from the terror that Locanas brought.

I remember the first time I saw him. He was trudging through the woods, and I was chasing after Soleil. He took one look at me, and then pounced. I screamed. I fought. I flailed. I was no match for his strength. He simply threw me over his shoulder like I was a sack of potatoes.

His hand on my butt, holding me in place. He was cruel. Uncaring. And of all the girls, he wanted only me.

A crash of thunder claps outside, and I cry out. Throwing the covers back, I leap for the door through the dimness, almost crippling when I put weight on my hurt ankle, I recover and then I'm grappling for the knob. When I find it, I turn it and push the door wide open, hobbling down the hall.

I push my tears out of the way, desperate to find Barre's room. There's another door a few feet from mine, so I test my luck and reach for it.

Before I can even open it, it swings open, revealing a shirtless Barre towering over me. His two different colored eyes are awake and alert as ever. He must have heard me, and nothing seems to get past this hunter man

I guess that means that he would notice if someone broke in. That brings me a lot of comfort.

"I'm sorry, I couldn't sleep, I'm too scared." I tell him, wrapping my arms around myself to keep from throwing myself into his room.

He just sort of looks down at me, his muscles tensed and his eyebrows furrowed. I look away. Embarrassment flutters in me, growing to display across my face.

Another tear spills, and when I go to swipe it from existence, my hand encounters another battling for it's place. I glance up at Barre as he places his thumb on my cheek, gathering the tear on the pad of his finger as he swipes it.

He's standing so close to me. I stare at his pecs, his dark nipples. I gulp. I should not be ogling him. Just because Barre is half naked does not give me permission to be creepy.

"I'll just go back to bed." I murmur, trying to back up. I need to go to my room, even if I don't want to. He follows me with thunderous stomps. I glance down to see he's barefoot, I guess he's just heavy.

Barre latches onto my shoulders, once again steering me. This time, he's pulling me into his room. I want to sob with relief. It's too good to be true.

He closes the door behind us, and then walks into the dark room. I stand anxiously, not able to see a thing. I limp further into the room, using my hands to feel for anything in the way.

A light clicks on, and I see that Barre stands by a small lamp on the nightstand. It hardly illuminates the room, but I can see enough.

The room is spacier than the one I was in, the bed much bigger. It's thick, wooden logs are covered in pelts, and there's a fireplace on the far right wall. There's no fire in it, but there's lots of firewood stacked beside it.

I near the bed, it's solid wood, made out of thick tree branches. The dark covers that match are rumpled from someone sleeping in them. I watch that someone very carefully. He pulls the blanket back, gesturing to it.

I get closer, standing beside him before climbing onto the cush mattress. The bed is high, so I have to throw my leg over to pull the rest of my weight up. Barre's hand goes to my elbow, helping me up. I gulp.

The sheets are still warm. The pillows are soft, molding perfectly to my head. I sigh in content.

Barre slides in beside me, turning off the light, showering us in darkness. I feel his closeness, the heat of his skin. I want to move closer.

He starts to shift, and I freeze, holding my breath. He's so near that if I reach out I'll touch him. So, I do. My fingertips make contact with hot, hard skin and muscle. My breath catches.

Barre doesn't move away. So I slowly creep closer, wanting to feel him, wanting to be completely safe.

Finally, he wraps an arm around me, pulling me to his body. I don't protest. I want this. I need it.

Being in his grasp, I'm so secure. It's like Locanas disappears when Barre is here. I don't worry about being kidnapped, I don't hang onto every sound, my heart doesn't gallop from my scared thoughts.

I close my eyes, already drifting to a peace filled sleep that I've been craving for years.

Chapter 7

Barre

I sleep better than I ever have with this tiny creature nestled in my arms.

No dreams of the past, no crippling fear of the further. Just peace. Warmth. Security.

I wake with Elodie snuggle up against my check, eyes shut and face calm. She makes little sounds in her sleep. I nestle my face into her neck and thick hair, taking a deep whiff of her

She's so soft. Her skin is without any texture or scars, it's just smooth and creamy and perfect. What lays beneath the skin is even more magnificent.

There's no muscle tone, just fat. It's squishy and malleable and plush beneath my hungry hands, and I want to feel more of it. It unlocks a primitive side of me that I never knew existed.

I want to have her in my nest ever night. I want her in my den every day. In my arms any time I want.

The list of impossible things I desire goes on. I want to keep Elodie, and the thought scares me. I have to keep control of myself. She must be returned to the palace, where she'll be happy, and safe.

I may be able to provide for myself, but I am no rich male. Only the wealthy can afford to pamper a female the way she needs. My Pa constantly spoke of how Mama complained if she wasn't provided with jewels and fine clothes, because she deserved the best.

I was young, but I remember how unhappy my Mama was at times. I couldn't stand to see Elodie that upset. It would bring so much shame, more than I already feel.

The thought of keeping her for myself, having her as a mate, it's so tempting that I consider it over and over. The palace would come looking. They would not simply forget about her. They would not rest until they had her.

Would they take her away if I already mated her? If my kit grew in her womb?

The idea sends a jolt through me, and I don't know what to think of it. The picture of little Elodie with a large belly filled with my offspring, I like it too much.

I realize I need to get out of this nest before I convince myself into abandoning my plan.

Detangling myself from the female, I let myself stare at her for a moment before I leave her. She sleeps so soundly. She's so beautiful. I want to reach out and touch her, stroke her red hair. I hold myself back.

I need to build a fire to keep Elodie warm, and I can't wake her. She needs rest.

I create a fire in my room, trying my best to stay quiet as I fill the fireplace with wood. The warmth spreads as I brush the splinters from my hands.

Standing, I shoot one last glance at the female. She's snuggled up tight in my nest, holding a pillow to her chest. No sign of her frightful self from last night.

My chest aches at the sight, and I rub the skin over my heart, wondering why I am experiencing these feelings.

I slip out of my nesting room silently, into the living space where I build another fire to warm the den. It roars to life, and I nod in satisfaction before moving to the kitchen.

I begin making breakfast, cracking open a few warak eggs and cooking them on the stove. I slice some meat and warm a few pieces of bread. I'm determined to make a good meal for this new little female that has entered my life suddenly.

Although I know I'm going to be trekking to the palace to bring her back, in the back of my mind I hope to impress her. Maybe she will want to stay. Maybe she will want me to provide for her as her mate.

Again, I shake my head at my own thoughts. They are impossible notions. I can never have a mate. I am not worthy of something so wonderful. I am destined to spend the rest of my life alone.

I've always been at peace with the idea of being alone, I enjoy have a quiet and predictable life, don't I? After finding Elodie, I'm not so sure anymore.

The wooden planks that make up the floor creak down the hall as a door opens. I'm just about finished making breakfast when Elodie hobbles into the kitchen.

She looks sleepy, rubbing her eyes and smoothing her very messy red hair. I can tell she just woke, but came straight to me. She's as beautiful as always.

The human looks at the food, and then looks at me.

"Go sit, the food is almost ready." I tell her, pointing at the table with authority. She should not be walking with her injured ankle, but I let it slide. I'm too distracted by her cuteness.

The little thing has the nerve to roll her eyes at me.

"arrant yew misstur bossie pants?" She mumbles, laughing to herself as she sits in the same chair she occupied last night.

Last night. I could not believe that she came to my room. I was shocked. After the thunder persisted, I heard her jump out of bed. It woke me. By the time I opened my own door, she was standing right outside my nesting room sheepishly.

I knew she wanted to sleep with me, but was too shy to ask. She almost went back to her own room, terror still shining in her green eyes. I couldn't have that. So, I took her in and put her in my own nest. I fell asleep with her cradled in my arms.

It was an experience unlike any other.

I dish up the food, coming to the table to serve the female. She stares at it with hungry eyes, watching the plate with interest. I suddenly feel envious of the food.

What is wrong with me?

Once she begins eating, I know I must get started running her a bath. I make sure she will stay put as I go to the bathroom. Elodie chews slowly, watching me as I leave.

I kneel by the large tub, turning the faucet until warm water shoots out, filling the bath. I check to make sure that the water is nice and hot before returning to the female. It makes me nervous to leave her alone for too long.

Even last night. I regretted leaving her by herself in my Pa's room. Not only for her comfort, but for mine. I need to know that she's safe, and when she's in my arms, I'm sure that she is.

Elodie is still in the kitchen when I get back, still eating with measured bites. I make myself a bowl of breakfast as well, eating it as quickly as possible. I don't want to waste a second of time.

"callm dowun. yewrr goin tooo choke." She admonishes me, scowling cutely with her lips pouting out.

I chuckle, slowing my eating as I'm assuming that's what she's going on about. Once she's appeased, she goes back to eating.

We both eat in silence for awhile, and I watch her carefully, hardly focused on my food at all. She's so perfect just sitting there. I could stare at her all day, but she must be bathed. And that is something I will not be watching.

I didn't have time to get her clean last night, too worried about her injuries and getting her to sleep. But, now she needs to be washed up. I don't know how long she was in the woods, but there's bound to be dirt on her.

"Okay, if you're done, it's time for a bath. Come." I say, realizing that she's finished her breakfast. Her orange eyebrows scrunch up, and I know that she doesn't understand me, but I love seeing that lost look on her face.

I reach cautiously for her hand, and she lets me take it. I hold her cold, small fingers in my own, staring at her pale nails.

Leading her away from the kitchen, I take Elodie into the bathroom where hot water continues to fill the bathtub. I let go of her hand, already missing her touch, and go to turn off the faucet. The flood shuts off, drops of excess water still dripping out.

"yew'r sew sweeet! thanck yew!" She remarks in excitement, dipping a hand into the water to test the temperature. She begins hopping up and down in excitement despite her hurt ankle.

I reach for her, trying to hold onto her should so she won't jostle her injury. As soon as I touch her, she pounces, wrapping me up in her thin, soft arms.

For a moment, I am frozen, having no idea what to do. Before I can return her embace, she lets go, red hair flying as she races to get undressed.

My eyes widen as she pulls at her dress, trying to tear it off. Once again I grab her. She looks up at me with questions in her eyes. I point to her bandage, and then her ankle. She nods in understanding.

I go onto one knee, making quick work of her bandage and her wrappings. I need to redress the wound as soon as she's done bathing. With the tips of my fingers, I carefully examine the cut on her arm. It's not as irritated anymore. The ointment seems to be doing it's job.

When I stand to leave, Elodie goes back to taking off her clothing, disinterested in the fact that I might catch a glimpse of her exposed skin.

I want to, oh how I want to see her without that dress in the way, but I will not. She has put her trust in me, and I won't betray it.

For now, I will have to focus on getting her fresh new clothes and a warm towel. It will be enough to keep my mind busy. At least, I hope that it will.

Chapter 8

Elodie

The next few days fly by, and I love every single minute of it. At least, I love every minute I spend with Barre.

When I'm left alone I start to get antsy. I glance out the windows, pulling the curtains closed to protect myself from the thought of Locanas. The fear of him seems to be more dangerous than the threat of the guy himself. I'm shocked he hasn't shown up yet. But the shadow of him still continues to loom over me.

I half expect him to bang down the door, demanding that Barre hand me over.

But after being around him, I know he wouldn't do that. He's sweet. Wonderful. Everything I've ever dreamed of, and more.

The big guy is pretty quiet, and stoick. His face is always so serious. Barre is the strong, silent type I've come to learn. But he seems to like me. He prioritizes me, and that doesn't go unnoticed. It's a rare thing, on Earthat least.

Every morning I wake up with an empty bed and the memory of his arms around me. I hobble to the kitchen where a hot, delicious breakfast awaits. He guides me to the table and serves me food while he redresses my wounds. His touch is always so careful and measured, and I can't seem to take my eyes off of him.

Barre makes me feel lazy with how much he does for me. But, he makes it look so easy, so effortless. And it's as if he doesn't mind one bit. He keeps the fires going, making the house warm constantly. He's gentle, but so big that it would seem impossible to be so careful. And yet, I don't doubt his strength.

I wake up this morning with a grin. After a few days of sitting inside, curiosity has been growing inside of me, and I suddenly want to look around. Of course, Barre is gone from the bed and the aroma of food being cooked travels through the house like every other morning.

I've been here for awhile, but I haven't seen Barre's pet since he carried me in through the front door. The dog-like creature didn't come into the house with us. He left it outside. I want to see it again, and sneaking outside is the only way to go.

It's not lost on me that the animal saved me. Without it, I wouldn't have been discovered by Barre. Who knows how long I would've been trapped out there, or what would've happened to me. I shiver at the thought. That dog deserves my appreciation.

So, I slide out of bed silently so my Rytarian warrior won't notice. He likes to keep an eye on me, and I have a feeling that he wouldn't want me outside. I'll have to be sneaky.

I pull at one of the many blankets piled high on the bed, wrapping the soft thing around my shoulders and tiptoeing down the hall and towards the front door. I check around the corner, making sure that I can't see Barre. He's nowhere to be seen.

I know the dog is outside on the porch. I've seen him or her walking around outside the window. He paces and sniffs, treading it's territory with it's head held high.

My curiosity grows as I reach for the front door. I look over my shoulder at the sounds that still echo from the kitchen. Barre hasn't noticed my secret mission yet, so I count that as a win.

The door knob isn't exactly silent when I click it to the side. It's a little chilly this morning, but it's comfortable. The hardwood of the porch creaks underneath my bare feet, the thick wood is damp under my cold toes, but I continue my pursuit. The trickling of rain is constant all around me, but the sound is nothing compared to the fierce growl that pierces the air.

The beast runs up to me, eyes blazing. It's so big and scary that my automatic reaction is to take a step back out of reluctance.

The dog-like monster stops suddenly in front of me, brown and white fur raised in alarm as it sniffs at me with his muzzle. It's head goes to my shoulders, taller than any canine I've seen. The small, black horns on it's head point backwards and run almost completely parallel to it's skull.

It's cute, with floppy ears and thick, plush fur. It's also scary. Red eyes, sharp teeth, huge paws. It's practically two of me.

Eventually it's growling ends rather abruptly. It's tail begins wagging and it bends it's head, nuzzling my hand with it's long snout.

I begin petting it, and it's purr is back again. It sounds like a huge cat. It rubs it's massive head against my open palm.

"Good boy. Who's a good boy?" The truth is I don't know if it's a boy or a girl. I sneak a peak on the underside of its body to see a definite sign of male-hood between his legs.

Definitely a boy then.

The dog turns, rubbing the side of his body on me as I continue scratching his coat all the way down his back. He's clearly enjoying the affection. I'm glad that he likes me, it would be pretty scary if he hated me. He could easily kill me if he wanted to.

"You're just a big ole sweet heart, aren't you?" I try to refrain from the baby talk, but I can't help it. This giant dog is so sweet, despite his appearance. His fur is soft, and he smells like the woods. He doesn't have a speck of dirt on him either. I like his ruggedness.

It just reminds me of his owner.

As if summoned by my thoughts, the front door swings open, making me jump, and Barre steps out into the drizzly morning, feet stomping.

The Rytarian has a disapproving look on his face as he watches me with his pet. I notice that Barre glances at my shoeless feet and growls low in his throat, shaking his head. I roll my eyes at him.

"Dupeshma Relinkas." He mutters, stepping forward to my side. I shrug. The language barrier is frustrating sometimes, but it doesn't make communication completely impossible.

"How come you leave this sweet guy out here all the time?" I wonder out loud, patting the dog on the back as his tail continues to wag happily. "It doesn't seem fair."

Barre grunts.

"Salsh." He calls, and the dog's ears perk up. He runs over to Barre, sitting at his feet, ears raised and eyes wide with attention. I'm guessing that's his name.

"Salsh." I replicate the word, and Barre stares at me with surprise in his eyes as the dog runs back to me. Before I know it, I'm being assaulted with slobbery dog kisses all over my face.

I laugh, pushing at his chest as the licks keep coming, he's too strong for me to push away. I hear a deep chuckle that sends a tingle down my spine. Even Barre's laugh is sexy. I haven't heard him do that. I could get used to that.

Salsh is pulled backwards by his collar, and I see Barre effortlessly holding his pet back. He shakes his head, watching his dog. I take the opportunity to admire his arm muscles as he holds Salsh's collar with one hand. The veins make me want to drool a little bit.

"Ashba dars relinkas yatushla." He admonishes, and the dog cocks his head to the side, as if even he understands what Barre says.

He claps him on the head, releasing his hold, and the animal runs off the deck and into the yard. I watch him disappear around the house with a bit of sadness. I nervously glance back at Barre, feeling somewhat guilty for coming outside without him knowing or without permission.

He gets closer to me, and I scoot back, wondering what he'll do next. Barre isn't looking at me. Instead, he's looking to where his dog ran.

Heavy hands land on my shoulders, and his thumb gently caresses the place between my neck and shoulder, his palm traveling upward. I shiver, a brief shot of desire shooting down my spine. I'm not used to that feeling. As much as I check him out, I rarely feel horny.

"Relinkas, destri massa trelip." He murmurs tenderly, and I raise my eyebrows as if the only reason I can't understand him is because I wasn't paying attention.

He's so warm, so inviting. I lean into him. I'm constantly realizing that I'm becoming increasingly obsessed with him. His hand is still caressing my neck, travelling across my shoulder gently. Barre tilts his head to the cabin with his thick neck, and I get the message.

"Okay, bossy." I sigh. Bossy is the best fitting nickname I've found for my rescuer. And that's what he is. He rescued me. From Locanas, from the cold and the dark. I would be lost without him. But, he is very bossy. I guess I'm okay with that.

And that's another thing, even as I walk into the safe haven that is Barre's bungalow, a chill creeps up my spine when I remember Locanas. I can still feel his breath washing over me, his enormous, wandering grip that traced my curves without permission.

Barre notices me stop in the foyer, he closes the door and quickly goes back to touching me. He's extremely touchy. I like it. Maybe too much. His touch, its so different from Locanas. He's so different from Locanas.

He seems to sense my fear, because he grabs my hand in his. I pause, relishing the feel of his rough fingertips scratching against me.

Wordlessly, Barre leads me into the kitchen to shove more food in my mouth. The man is always feeding me like his life depends on it. I can't complain. I love to eat, and he's an amazing cook.

But I can't focus while I eat, or while the day disappears, quickly turning into night. All I can think of is Barre. I stare at him constantly, enamoured by him. It amazes me that someone so large can move so fluidly. And his scars and facial hair, they make his sharp face mysterious and so handsome that I can't drag my gaze away from him.

Finally, the sun sets. The day went by fast, but its not always like that. Because the night is my favorite. Some days I spend hours waiting around as Barre does chores. I follow him wherever he goes, carefully observing and trying to help where I can.

I just love going to bed for the night. It's the best part of all of it. I get to hold him, and he holds me right back.

Barre draws me a bath, as he does every night. I quickly run through the process of scrubbing and rinsing every inch of my body with his bar of soap. The water is hot and refreshing, and I like the idea of being nice and clean before bed.

I get dressed in one of Barre's shirts, which is more than a dress on me. It makes me feel like a child. But the fabric is so soft, and it just smells like him.

When I get to his bedroom, he's standing at the window, staring out into the pitch black night. He turns when he hears me enter the room. I freeze, standing in the doorframe with my arms crossed.

He's shirtless. Again. I gulp, trying to look anywhere but his rock hard 6-pack and the v shaped curve of his hips. He finally moves, for which I'm glad. He lifts the covers off the bed, taking a small, unsure step back.

I rush forward, fully aware of the excitement I display when I can't control myself. I can't help it though.

Curling up in the covers, I moan at the warmth and comfort of the bed. I glance up to see Barre standing over me with a darkness in his mismatched eyes. I gulp, suddenly nervous that I've done something wrong. He flicks the light off, and it takes my eyes a second to adjust.

To gain back his favor, I open my arms wide in an obvious invitation for him to join me. He freezes, seeming like he can't move a single muscle as he stares down at me.

Before I know it, he's climbing over me and letting my arms wrap around his warm, hard body.

Barre sighs into my hair, groaning as his muscles release their tension. The dark consumes me, and I feel myself relax. When I'm here, I feel unbelievably safe, like nothing can hurt me ever again.

I can't help but wonder if this is what I've been waiting for all along.

Chapter 9

Barre

I stare at the food in my hands, wieghing it in each palm. I decide it would be better to be safe, and I fold the rest of the food into a cloth wrap and push it into my bag.

The past day I have done hardly anything but pack for the long journey to the palace. Elodie is completely oblivious to my need to prepare for our trek. She watches me come and go with clothing and first aid supplies, cute red eyebrows raised in curiosity. Intelligent eyes following my every move.

She probably is wondering what took me so long to bring her back to her rightful place. I have to admit that she acts as if she's content here. Despite my little den and lack of pampering, I have done everything I can to make her comfortable.

Elodie has shown no sign of being upset by my home or food. In fact, she often smiles at me like there's no place she'd rather be. I know that it's impossible. It must be because she's a "human". Or, she is just trying to make me feel better about what I lack.

I wouldn't be surprised. She is sweeter than any creature I've met. She snuggles up to me like a kit in my nest, I wake up to her petting my hair and running her nails over the back of my neck.

Most times, this warrants a reaction from my body. I cannot help the excitement that shoots through my veins at the slightest touch from the female. All of it is new. I don't mind it.

I haven't received affection since my Mama succumbed to the infection that took all the females. I didn't realize what I had been missing.

As a gladiator, the only interaction with flesh I had was pain, or causing hurt. But now, now I touch her back, my fingertips gentle. I cannot be too careful with Elodie's thin skin and soft body. I cringe to think how easy it would be to inflict an injury on her.

That's why I can't keep her. I am a rough fighter, a rugged mountain dweller with no knowledge of how to keep a mate. How to make a female happy. How to raise kits.

A deep, throbbing sorrow erupts in my chest. I run a frustrated hand through my hair, hating the helpless feeling that follows and clings to me.

Latching the bag, I pat it in approval. I packed everything relatively quickly. I'm happy with what I've accomplished in a short time. Having Elodie here has inhibited me from hunting, or walking my forest. I have a lot of land that I own, and I like to keep it maintained.

But I can't leave her here. And she seems to have an unusual reaction to the woods. She gets an odd look on her face when she stares out at the trees. It gives me an unsettled feeling. I want to protect her and comfort her in any way that I can, but how can I do that when I don't know what it is that troubles her?

"Barre." My voice being called alerts me to the little she standing in my kitchen with a smile on her face. As always, time seems to slow to a stop when I spot her.

"What is it, tiny?" I wonder, grabbing my bag off the counter and walking closer to her.

The nickname is something that I thought was funny at first, but it stuck. It fits her.

"waat aryew do-en?" She asks, coming closer to tug on my arm that is likely as long as she is.

I roll my eyes playfully, putting a hand on top of her head and moving it from side to side. I don't know the words she asked, but I can guess, and I don't have to endure any embarrassment if I get it wrong because she cannot understand me either. It just feels comforting to talk to her.

"I am packing for our trip. It's time to put you where you belong." The admission dampens my happy mood at seeing Elodie. She notices.

Her pretty face falls. The brown spots scrunch in between her red eyebrows. I cannot get over her appearance at times. Red hair. It is unheard of in my kind. Maybe all humans have red hair. I don't like the thought of that. Without thinking, I reach over and pinch a wavy lock of her hair in between my fingers. I don't like the thought of the color being generic. Elodie is anything but generic, I'm sure of it.

"I will miss you, tiny." I sigh, not knowing what to do with all of the emotions bubbling up inside of me. A gladiator doesn't have emotions. No empathy, no sorrow, no love.

Maybe I am not what I always thought that I was. I have so many thoughts and feelings that I've never experienced before now that she's here. I wonder if they will disappear with her.

But I don't want her to leave, quite the opposite, even if it is what's best. It feels like she belongs here in my heart, in my den, in my nest. She's become a part of my daily life, and I don't want to let her go.

I take Elodie's hand in mine, it feels so perfect, like our hands meld together. She trustingly follows after me, watching calmly as I grab my supplies and take her out of the den.

The sun shines brightly outside. It's rare weather, but I appreciate the warmth it brings.

I glance down at my human when she tugs on my hand. She's trembling, looking around at the bright green nature around us. I'm not shocked at her reluctance, I knew it would be there. She's afraid of the woods.

And it's no surprise why. When I found her she was hurt and scared, alone in a tree and waiting for something to end her. The memory of the sight still makes my heart ache.

"There's no reason to be afraid, tiny. I will protect you here. There is no other on this planet that matches my power." It's not something I point out often, but I'm convinced that the information would comfort her if only she knew.

But Elodie can't understand me. It's something I have to keep reminding myself. It's just so frustrating that there's such a lack of communication between us.

It won't matter soon.

"Salsh!" I call, squeezing the human's little fingers in reassurance. I know how she loves the rasler, and how he takes to her as well.

It's odd, my pet doesn't like anyone but me, but he almost prefers Elodie to his own master.

He comes sprinting around the corner, tail wagging as soon as he sees the female. He trots right up to her side and nuzzles her wrist. She pets his ear, scratching behind his horn but keeping a firm grip on me with her other hand.

I check to make sure that the door to my den is locked, and that everything is as it should be. I pull Elodie off the porch behind me, stepping onto the trail that I know by heart.

It usually takes me a sun cycle or two to make the journey, but I would guess that Elodie being with me will take longer. She's still limping, her ankle not completely healed just yet,

We will have to take it slow. I would rather wait until it's better to take her on a long trek, but she's healing much slower than any Rytarian. I don't know how long it will take. And the technology in the palace will help her get better faster.

Salsh follows at Elodie's side, and Elodie lets me lead her through the dense trees. I made sure that she dressed warm enough for the weather, but she's still shaking.

She must be shaking because of her fear. The idea troubles me, but knowing that she trusts me enough to follow me is enough to boost my confidence. Elodie makes me feel like I could do anything. I just hope that I won't let her down.

Chapter 10

Elodie

Barre has an enormous bag hanging over his shoulder. The thing looks heavy, but he carries it like it weighs absolutely nothing. I'm not surprised, but I'm confused. He's packed tons of stuff, and he looks like he means business.

It freaks me out, especially since we can't communicate. I wish I could ask him what he's doing, where we're going, why he's taking me away and into the wilderness.

We're in the middle of the woods, traveling far from his little cabin. It makes me nervous to be honest, but I trust Barre more than anyone. I'm just scared Locanas is gonna jump out from behind a tree and grab me.

Salsh nudges my hand, and I lift my arm to pat his head. He purrs happily and I finally feel relaxed enough to smile.

Being out in the woods again is rough. I stick close to Barre's back, letting him lead me through the thick foliage and trees, but struggling to keep up with him with my ankle and general slowness. He occasionally slows down to let me catch up with him, smiling kindly like he understands.

Since the last time I was in the woods I was running for my life I didn't have time to look around and appreciate the beauty of these alien woods. I glance all around, craning my neck and listening to each new sound that echoes off of the trees.

I imagine all the mysterious animals they have here, and the plants too. I've always loved flowers. I've yet to see any here, yet.

The forest feels alive under my feet, I half expect the ground to rise and fall with breath. The dirt and trees are still damp, even as the rain has finally stopped. There has to be flowers.

My shoes, sleek green flats from the palace, are caked in mud, and definitely not suited for this type of terrain. I wonder if I can get some better ones while I'm out here. I wonder where Barre gets all of his things.

I find myself wondering a lot of things that I wish could be cleared up. Unfortunately, neither of us can speak to one another. Huge bummer.

I want to know why we're out here exploring the landscape of Rytaria. I think it would make me more useful to know the purpose. I put my head down from the tree tops to watch Barre's large stride in front of me. He's always looking back to check on me. He's got that big old bow slung on his back, his bag on his shoulder. His big legs look muscular under his pants. He has no problem trudging along. He doesn't seem to get tired.

Maybe this is a hunting trip. I have the feeling that's what he was doing when he stumbled upon me. I feel bad for disrupting his plans. It makes me think I'm somewhat of a burden to him. That's the last thing I want to be. The first thing is his mate.

I've never met someone so tender, so sweet.

It's such a contrast to Locanas.

I suddenly wonder if anyone notices I'm gone. Obviously Soleil will, but the palace has loads of females, none of which have the red hair curse. They probably won't think twice that I'm missing.

And maybe that's a good thing. I can stay out here with Barre. I'll become his mate. If he wants me. He's sort of sending mixed signals. He's sweet, too sweet. Maybe it's because I'm female and he feels some sort of responsibility to take care of me. I wish it was because he felt something more for me, and not just my gender.

I don't exactly blame him. His kind is obsessed with anything that has boobs. I haven't been able to communicate with any of the Rytarian, beast like men, but I've heard enough from Soleil.

Is that why Barre is so tender with me? Why he's so protective and gentle? Does he feel drawn to the role of my defender simply because I'm a rare piece of meat?

Everything in me screams no, that can't be, I already feel like I know the guy. It's worth considering though.

My legs ache, my ankle giving me trouble. We've been taking the journey slow, a fact I attribute to the nurturing side of Barre. I can tell he's mindful of my human-ness. It doesn't take rocket science to determine that he's likely much stronger than me. And yet, he slows his pace to make sure I'm comfortable. It's very kind.

I stop, leaning against a tree as my twisted ankle twinges. I try to catch my breath, looking ahead to Barre, who has already stopped. Slash runs back to me, sniffing at my face. I smile softly, pushing away my fear of the woods for a moment.

"Can we stop?" I wonder aloud, knowing full well that he doesn't understand me in the slightest. The language barrier doesn't seem to stop me from talking Barre's ear off anyway.

Instead of answering me, the giant stalks towards me quickly, towering over me like the trees surrounding us.

"I just need a little time to rest, then I'll be good as ne.." I cut off mid sentence when he bends at the waist to pick me up by my hips.

I have a flashback, the combination of the forest and the movement has me wailing. Clutching at his shoulders, I try to pry myself away from him, tears springing to my eyes. It's too much, too similar to that day that Locanas grabbed me, slung me over his shoulder, and dropped me to the ground. I'm transported back to that day, all the pain and fear he caused me in that moment.

Before I can scream, I'm back on the ground. Barre's panicked, mismatched eyes are staring down at me as he grabs my face, frantically wiping away my tears. I hate the confusion in his expression. He's beyond worried.

I sniffle, feeling pathetic. Why did that stupid Rytarian have to damage me so much? Poor Barre, he doesn't deserve this. He's not Locanas. He's nothing like Locanas.

"I'm sorry, I'm so sorry." I beg, throwing myself around him. I burrow my face in his chest, and cry softly, wishing this could all be over.

He stands there for a few moments, complaining still as stone. Slowly, his arms come down to wrap around me. I swear I've never felt so safe in my whole life.

Chapter 11

Barre

I walk carefully through the forest, each step calculated as to not disrupt the precious creature cradled in my arms.

Elodie tired herself out crying. She promptly fell asleep as I held her. The poor thing gave me a fright when she panicked. All I did was try to pick her up to give her injured ankle a rest. She was tired, so carrying her would have been the obvious choice.

The fear in her voice, the trembling, the tears. It was too much. I didn't know what to do as she fell apart in my grasp.

My biggest question is, why did she act that way? What happened before to instill so much fear in Elodie?

The possibilities anger me. It doesn't seem right that someone as sweet as her should be afraid. If anyone has hurt her....the mere thought alone is enough to send me into a fury. I only hope she doesn't wake and have the same reaction as she did earlier.

I glance down at her as I stomp through the fading light of day. She slumbers peacefully, her cheek resting on her hand that's pressed to my chest. Every delicate breath in and out of her lungs has my attention.

Everything she does. Every small sound, word, movement, it all feels important. I pay close attention to her.

In all my cycles, I've never been more needed than I am with Elodie. Being a gladiator never felt this important, this fulfilling. Holding her, caring for her, it feels like the most important job I've ever done.

Returning her to the palace is the most noble thing I can do. Giving up this feeling won't be easy, but it's for the best. It's what Elodie needs.

Even Salsh has become attached. The rasler is worried about her. Whenever she's in distress, he's on high alert. I have no doubt that he would protect her with his life if it came down to it.

I'm sure he'll be disappointed when I return her to her rightful place. Not as disappointed as I'll be, but I'm used to the feeling.

I walk for a long time, stepping over obstacles carefully so as to not jostle the female. She doesn't wake, hardly even stirs. I have to resist watching her. It's very tempting, but I can't risk stumbling and waking her.

Thankfully, I know the way to the palace by heart. I travel there fairly often for supplies. It'll take a few rotations to get there because of Elodie and her injuries and weakness. I don't mind the delay, in fact I'd do anything to draw the trip out.

I keep an eye out for empty space, a meadow of some sort to build my tent for the night. Setting up a camp won't take much time, but finding a good place is the tough part. Usually when I travel, I sleep under the stars, but I won't let Elodie sleep on the hard ground or without shelter over her head.

Finally, I discover a valley of grass and wildflowers situated among the trees. I nod my head in approval as I find a soft place to lay the tiny female. I gently lower her into the cradle of grass. Elodie makes a soft mewl, curling into a ball for warmth as I release her. She doesn't wake, for which I'm grateful.

I stare down at the female for a few moments. Salsh trots up, nuzzling Elodie's wrist insistently. I snap my fingers at him. He glances up at me, and I shake my head once. He knows the signal of my disapproval.

Instead, he decides to lay down against the human, snuggling close to her until she wraps an arm around his torso. She nestles her face into his fluffy coat, sighing contently.

Salsh gives me a look of defiance, and I smile softly at him. It would seem he's outsmarted me.

I make quick work of building the tent structure, unraveling blankets for a makeshift nest. Once I'm satisfied, I go back to her, picking her up and carrying her to my tent. She smiles in her sleep, adorably.

By the time she's settled in the blankets, it's completely dark out. I feel ashamed that I didn't get the chance to feed her last meal. We stopped earlier to eat, but she needs to eat often to heal. I'm not doing very well at caring for her. I need to do better.

I sigh, shaking my head as I close the flap door, tying it shut. Salsh lays down outside, already snoring from the long day of traveling. I settle myself in front of Elodie, laying on my side and watching her in what little light remains from the moons.

She's beautiful. I pull the blankets up to cover her, all the way up to her neck. It gets cold at night, and I don't want her to catch a chill.

Elodie begins mumbling in her sleep. I grin to myself, she's done this before. We sleep in the same nest every night. When she's very tired, she says a few words. I don't understand them obviously, but it's cute regardless.

"no Locanas. juuust Barre." She rambles senselessly, clutching at the blanket while her red eyebrows furrow.

I recognize two names in the jumble of words. Mine, and another. I glower, my smile disintegrating. I don't know who this Locanas is, but I don't like the fact that she's saying his name. It's a Rytarian name. He must be from the Palace.

Momentarily, I wonder who this male is, and why Elodie is dreaming of him. At least she also said my name, that has to count for something.

I sigh, rubbing my tired face and reaching out to hold the tiny female.

"I'm here."

Chapter 12

Elodie

I stare down at the river with my eyes fixed on my prize, determination buzzing through me. I bite my lip in concentration.

The weird alien fish flits through the water, unaware of me and Barre's growling stomachs.

The giant stands behind me, watching on. I could tell that he wanted to do this. Some primal part of him refuses to let me do anything really. I made it clear towards him that I'm not some helpless creature. I want to help.

So, Barre gave in, and he showed me how to spear a fish. It's been a long day of walking through the woods once again, but I could only take a few hours before I got tired again. My back still hurts from sleeping in that tent last night.

I hold the short spear in my hand, watching and waiting as the alien fish swims closer and closer to me unsuspectingly. I glance back at the Rytarian for approval. He simply nods his head once, and I strike.

The blade dives down through the water and into the fish. I squeal in success. After what feels like a hundred failed attempts, I finally got one!

I pull the spear from the river and show Barre with a grin. The red, wriggling fish has sharp fins and beady, black eyes.

Barre smiles at me, a gentle smile without showing his teeth. It's an un-intimidating look of pride and encouragement that boosts my self esteem more than a little.

My alien man carefully takes the spear from my hands, placing a hand on my shoulder as he brings the skewered creature to his eyes for inspection. He towers over me, so it's hard to crane my neck as I watch him right behind me.

He narrows his eyes, taking a swift bite of the still moving fish.

I throw my hands over my mouth, trying not to throw up as I begin gagging.

Disgusting.

Barre raises his eyebrows at me in question, continuing to chew on the completely raw fish. He holds the slime covered fish to me, and I cringe, taking a step back and letting his hand fall from my shoulder.

"No sushi for me, thanks." I laugh, putting a hand to my stomach to try to settle it.

Obviously, the giant doesn't understand a single word that I say. I sigh, shaking my head in frustration. This might take some time to communicate that I need to cook the meat in order to eat it.

An hour, and lots of hand signs later, we have a large fire going. Well, Barre has a large fire going. He's extremely resourceful in the outdoors.

I'm wrapped up tight in a blanket, seemingly useless beside my fish catching. I'm thankful for the heat from the fire. It's cold out tonight, especially still being damp from the river. I tried drying off, but the water seems to stick.

I sit back on my heels, watching carefully as Barre cooks the fish over the flame. He caught a few more after my successful catch as well, all of which he ate raw, straight out of the river.

The fire is large, atleast 5 feet tall. It's kind of scary.

Salsh lays next to me, equally enamoured with the food and all of the aromas coming from it. It doesn't smell fishy, for which I'm grateful.

Finally, after what feels like forever, he takes the fish from the fire. He offers it to me, putting his hand on my back as I hold the spear, inspecting the now cooked fish.

"Relinkas, shasa, felivf." He murmurs, I look at him in confusion. He then makes an eating motion. I sigh, nerves wracking me. I've never been good at trying new things, specifically strange foods.

I close my eyes, leaning forward and taking a small, unsure bite of the thing, testing the flesh on my tongue. I chew slowly, realizing that it's delicious. It doesn't really taste like any fish or meat that I've ever eaten on Earth, but it's not half bad.

It tastes kind of spicy, and almost fresh like a vegetable. It's an odd combination that I'm not mad about.

"Mmm. It's good." I tell Barre, smiling so he knows that I'm praising him. He smiles back, another soft lift of the corner of his lips. His blue eye and brown eye are both beautiful, they always take my breath away.

I take a few more hearty bites, licking my fingers as I pull off some smaller pieces. I'm almost completely full when Salsh whines beside me. I look at him, his red eyes pleading. I grin, offering him a large piece. He grabs it, as if he's scared I'll change my mind.

The alien dog runs off with the food, darting behind the tent to enjoy his meal.

I yawn, deciding it's time for bed. I stand up, stretching my arms over my head. I try to take a step, but the combination of my hurt ankle and the long blanket have me stumbling. I try to regain my footing, but it's too late. I'm already falling fast, right towards the bonfire.

There's no time to scream in terror before I'm being grabbed. Barre pulls me away from the roaring flames. The momentum sends me down against him, falling across his chest. He holds me to him, worry painted across his face.

"yetlee careesta, misha." He says to me, his voice rougher than it usually is, but still so sweet. I can see the strain he's inhibiting.

He's been calling me misha a lot lately, and I wonder what it could possibly mean.

"Sorry." I breathe, right before murmuring a "thank you."

He just saved my life for the second time, no big deal.

It's not lost on me that I'm laying across him, my body completely parallel to his. His body feels like it's sculpted out of marble, rock hard and perfect. He's staring at me. I'm staring at him. My eyes flick down to his full lips, and I feel an ache bloom inside of me.

Before I can think, I grab his face and put my mouth on his.

I've never kissed someone, never been kissed, so the feeling is odd. I know what to do instinctively. I move my lips against his, and for a moment he's stagnant. I move against him anyway, arching my back until my breasts are pressed against his chest. I moan when his tongue is suddenly in my mouth. Barre is kissing me back with a vengeance.

His hand is harsh on my hip, his other hand palming my skull and he pulls me even closer towards him. He groans, sounding like he's unraveling like me. I can hear my own breath as we tangle in passion.

Barre's kiss is hot and possessive. Despite his appetite for raw fish, his mouth tastes good, just as good as he smells.

Heat grows between us as we build a fire of our own, the other flame completely forgotten as the night takes a turn for the better.

My tongue tenderly battles his, his ferocious perusal matching my own. After what feels like an hour of fleeting time, he releases me.

His lips are swollen now, his eyes lit with excitement and curiosity. Barre's strong hand is still plastered to my hip, holding me firmly as pets my face with fascinated fingers.

My heart is thudding like crazy in my chest. I can't believe I did that. I've never had that much courage before. I'm oddly proud of myself.

I grin up at Barre, and I want to kiss him all over again, but restrain myself. He pulled away from me. He didn't seem upset, but I'm not going to push it if he was the one to put a stop to it.

Just when I thought he was indifferent to me, he returned my kiss. I guess he does like me after all. I wonder to myself if this means we're mates now, or on our way to becoming mates.

Barre makes a gruff sound in his throat, staring deep into my eyes. Soon, he gestures to the tent, and I huff. The sun is setting, and he wants me to sleep.

I try to climb off of him, but my ankle twinges in protest, and I suck in a breath of pain. Okay, so that was a bad angle.

My alien giant is quick to swing me up into his arms. I cling to his neck as he goes to the fire, stomping it into coals with his boot. My eyes widen, watching him as he nods in satisfaction before turning back to the tent, carrying me effortlessly.

Barre crawls into the tent, tucking me into the sea of blankets, his head lightly touching my temple as he checks me over. He pauses briefly to tie the flap closed and comes back to me. I'm laying on my back, staring up at the dark tent ceiling.

Usually I'm pulled tightly to his side while I sleep, but today he simply lays his head on my chest, his strong arms winding around my waist as he nestles himself into my stomach.

My mind goes hazy for a second, feeling way too warm to think. So, I do what comes naturally, I put my fingers in his thick, black hair. I run my fingernails softly against his scalp, messaging him as I think of a lullaby to sing.

This all reminds me of comforting my little siblings when they had bad dreams. I was always in a similar position, a head snuggled against my torso as I sang some sort of song to lull them back to sleep.

I remember one of my favorites, and begin singing.

"Stars shining bright above you
Night breezes seem to whisper 'I love you'
Birds singing in the sycamore tree
Dream a little dream of me."

I test my voice, finding it a little rusty, but Barre palms my back, silently encouraging me to continue. I clear my throat a bit before starting again.

"Say 'Nightie night' and kiss me
Just hold me tight and tell me you'll miss me
While I'm alone and blue as can be
Dream a little dream of me."

I yawn, my mouth goes wide, a signal of my exhaustion. I start to drift off, my dreams filled with the kiss that shook my whole world.

Chapter 13

Barre

I'm once again holding Elodie in my arms as I walk through the forest. She is still slow. I had no idea it would take this long for her to heal. Humans must heal at a much slower rate than Rytarians.

I feel incredibly guilty for traveling when she's still injured, but the palace has many healing remedies that she will have access to when she arrives. The sooner we get there, the better. I just wish I didn't contribute to her pain.

My mind wanders often to the kiss she gave me. I don't think I've ever felt so much desire, so much affection. I didn't want it to end, but I ended it anyway.

If I thought I was becoming attached before, I'm definitely attached now. The thought of giving up Elodie is unbearable.

I glance down at her cautiously. She holds a handful of flowers that she insisted on picking this morning. She won't stop raving over them, smiling as she touches their pedals gently.

When she started plucking them from the ground, she didn't even notice the Triperef behind her. I had raised my weapon, ready to take it down if it charged the precious human. Elodie was completely oblivious of the silent show down, too focused on the field of wildflowers around her to see the danger.

The beast wasn't large for its species, and it didn't seem aggressive, in fact it's snout twitched in curiosity. Sometimes triperefs can be antagonistic. This one simply trotted back into the woods. I had lowered my bow after that, convinced that the creature somehow knew of Elodie's importance.

By the time she was done gathering a bouquet, the beast was long gone, and I could finally relax. It is my job to make sure she's safe. I am bound by duty to protect any female, but Elodie has become more than that to me.

I stare down at her now, watching as she traces the many scars on my neck and chest, the skin that's exposed not quite covered by my shirt. She's become important to me because she's Elodie, she's so much more than just being a female.

She sings to me the past few nights, something I didn't expect. I love it. The last 2 nights have been filled with her songs. Her voice is melodic, entrancing.

It reminds me of when my own Mama would sing me to sleep at night. The presence of a female just has a way of making you feel right.

After lots of walking, it's time for a break, and to feed Elodie. I find a small creek, setting the human on a nearby boulder while I take off my bag, digging through the contents.

I take out the leftover Yaltrip, a food that Elodie calls "fsshh". Her words for things are always cute.

The female insisted that I cook the flesh, and I gladly did to keep her happy. I look down at the crisp food, wondering if it tastes any better than a fresh catch, I sincerely doubt it.

"fir-me?" She wonders, standing up. I hold a hand out, prepared for when she falls, and she does.

I've decided that Elodie is extremely clumsy, I'm not sure if it's because of her ankle or if it's simply in her nature.

"I always want to stay put, tiny, but you never do." I muse, close to chuckling at her. She never notices that she should stay put. It's frustrating.

She grins, putting her hands on my arms for support.

"thankyeww" She says, something she says often.

Salsh runs up, panting with energy as he nudges my side. I glance down to see a stick hanging from his mouth. He wants to play.

Elodie grabs for the stick, I take it from her hand, replacing the branch for the food. She shakes her head, taking a bite of it anyway. She knows that her eating pleases me.

I turn my attention to my pet. He jumps and leaps, ready for me to toss the stick. I do, throwing it far into the woods and watching him chase after it.

Elodie laughs.

I smile to myself, going back to my bag and taking out a rag, and dragging the cloth under the stream. The water is cool and refreshing, I cup some in my hand, bringing it to my lips. I decide that I need to fill my bottle before leaving here.

First, I need to address Elodie's wound.

"Tiny." I say, and she perks up, coming to me. She knows her nickname by now.

I lift the rag, and she knows what I'm planning to do. She takes another bite of the yaltrip while she walks.

I pull her into my lap, sitting her on my knee as I unwrap her dressing. The scratch on her arm is healing nicely. Although, if it was my wound it would've been gone by now.

I gently clean the deep scratch, pulling ointment from my pack and applying it to the gash carefully. I know it pains her at times, but my strong Elodie doesn't flinch. She grits her teeth and lets me do my work.

She may not be strong physically, but she's tough in my eyes. I find myself wondering what her threat level is. It can't be very high from what I've seen.

I'm typically very good at guessing a threat level, I always had to size up my opponent with calculating eyes. I was trained to assess threats.

Maybe she's a 10 or 15, I wouldn't be surprised if it was even lower than that.

Helpless little female. But she's resilient, I must give her that.

After I re-wrap her wound, I'm packing everything up once more. Elodie plays with Salsh, tugging at the stick he has in his mouth. He pulls it, dragging her to the ground in the process.

She shrieks, and I stand in alarm, only to realize that she's laughing.

Slash drops the stick, running to her and sniffing her face to make sure she's alright. He licks her cheek as she continues to giggle, reaching up to pet his neck.

Definitely below a threat level 15 I decide. Even Salsh is level 42.

"Elodie. Salsh." I call them, and they both look at me. "Time to go."

Salsh trots to my side, leaving Elodie on the ground to get up on her own. She struggles, and I immediately go to her side and pull her up gently.

"ya, ya." The human grumbles, dusting off her knees before straightening to her full height. She winks at Salsh before smiling up at me.

My heart twinges, and I feel the overwhelming urge to just pick her up and take her back to my cabin. We could have a happy life together. No one would have to know that I took her. It could be a secret.

I can certainly dream, but fantasy and reality just are not the same thing unfortunately. As much as I can try to convince myself I will make Elodie happy, it's simply not true.

I sigh, staring at the horizon. We're getting closer to the palace with every step. Soon, we'll be able to see the buildings towering above the trees. And then, we'll be at the palace gates. I'll have to turn Elodie over, and I'll likely never see her again.

It's my duty to look after her best interests, I just wonder why my chest aches when I think of leaving her there. I can't keep her, I just can't.

A heathen can't love. A heathen can't take care of a mate. Elodie deserves the world, and I only wish that I could be the one to give it to her.

Chapter 14

Elodie

I'm wiping sweat from my brow, looking up at the sun when I see it. A steeple, a tall metal point way up in the sky, brushing the dark clouds. The structure glistens in the sunlight, glinting into my eyes.

I sober at the sight, halting where I stand in the woods, several feet behind Barre. My lip starts to tremble, and I have to bite it to keep it from wobbling uncontrollably.

We're walking towards the steeple, which obviously belongs to the palace. He can't be taking me to the palace, can he?

Panic explodes inside of me. Why are we going so close to the palace? Are we going to the markets that are in the city? That has to be it. There would be no other reason to be here. No other explanation.

I look at my torn up shoes. I could use a new pair, that's for sure. Maybe he noticed. Barre is sweet like that.

The fear of being there causes my heart to stutter.

I continue trekking on anyway, pushing at the giant's arms when he tries to pick me up. I'm so tired of him treating me like that. I want to show him that I'm not weak and helpless like he seems to think I am.

It's not that I'm ungrateful for his constant help, but I just don't like being seen as less in any capacity. I've been treated like dirt enough in my life so far.

I look up at Barre and his pitch black hair, wondering if he looks at my own red locks and sees me as inferior, just like everyone else has for so long. I touch my red hair on top of my head, it's pulled into a ponytail to keep it out of my face.

Subconsciously, my fingertips brush my freckle dotted face. Barre never stared at them with disgust. Maybe he's good at disguising it? Everyone on Earth, besides Soleil, despised the way I look. Why would Rytaria be any different?

He notices that I've slowed down, and that I'm touching my face. He smiles, walking back to me and cupping my face the way he so often does. I try to smile back at him, but I find it difficult with the foreboding in my gut.

That's why. That's why Rytaria is different. How could I have forgotten? Barre is so completely opposite of what I've known men to be on Earth. How could I have compared him to them?

Salsh nudges my hand, wanting pets as always. I give in. He basks in the affection, his tongue hanging out happily and I run my hand up and down this head, flipping his ears.

I can't lose Barre. I can't lose Salsh. They're all I have now.

My mind wanders as we continue to walk endlessly. I trip over tree roots, rocks, and twisting foliage. Barre keeps grabbing in my arm to steady me, his big hand on the small of my back in a reassuring touch.

He's still been carrying me occasionally, but my ankle actually feels a lot better now. I've been keeping up with his fast pace more than usual.

A bird call squawks overhead, a strange noise that I'm not prepared for. I jump slightly.

It reminds me of back home in Tennessee. Soleil and I would spend hours in the woods. I miss her. My heart jolts in my chest at the reminder. I may miss her, but I can't see her. If I see her I risk seeing another face that occupies the palace.

The idea terrifies me, and I trip. Of course, Barre thinks that the misstep was due to my injury, and he's quick to fuss over me.

"Misha, ebsee yantriskii." He murmurs, and I brush him off.

"I'm not a baby, Barre." I laugh, because to him I probably am a baby. I glance up at him, and he smiles. His display of joy makes my lungs freeze up. He's so handsome with his mismatched eyes.

I can picture myself waking up to him every morning for the rest of my life. I have come to realize that I already think of him as my mate.

Does he feel the same way? Curse our stupid language barrier.

But I can't help but feel like every touch, every movement towards me is deliberate on his part. He has to care for me, no one would treat someone like this if they didn't care.

And Soleil was very clear about how barbaric they are. Once they see you as their mate, it's difficult to convince them otherwise. I've learned that to be true from Locanas. Maybe Barre thinks I'm already his mate.

My spirit brightens at the thought, and I never thought I'd feel this happy. I grab his much larger hand, brushing the tan skin with my thumb. I let him lead me, trusting where he's leading me.

Maybe things are finally looking up for me after all.

Chapter 15

Barre

When I wake the next day, a deep pit of despair fills my stomach. I dress quickly, being silent as I stare down at the beautiful female sleeping in the nest of furs and pillows I have provided for her. I remember the past few nights with burning fondness.

Fingers in my hair, sweet words drifting through the air. To be with Elodie is to love her.

Her red hair is sprawled out, her brown fleck covered face is soft and peaceful with her slumber. She has no worries, knowing that I'll watch over her.

I try not to dwell on what will happen today. I must enjoy the short, precious time that I have with my sweet Elodie. Only, she's not mine, I have to remind myself of this over and over again. She never was mine, and she never will be.

Tracing the tips of my fingers across her pale cheek, I clench my jaw. She deserves someone better, someone without scars and death, a male with a tender nature. I am not pure enough to enjoy her.

She will likely mate to one of the Emperor's warriors, someone of a high and noble rank. I imagine her smiling at someone else and the thought alone causes my muscles to tense in upset. I can't even begin to think of her sweet mouth on someone else'a lips.

Leaving her side, I begin packing up the camp as quietly as possible to keep my mind from wandering. My attempt to be inconspicuous is in vain. The slight noises of my packing wake her. She props herself up on her elbow, grinning up at me sleepily, melting my heart. She rubs at her green eyes.

"gud mrning." She murmurs, and I smile sadly. These are the last times I will hear her odd language spoken in her beautiful voice.

She has no idea what my plan is, but I can only hope that she will go along with it. Returning her had been the plan all along, so why do I feel as if my heart is being ripped from my chest?

The amount of injuries I have had in the arena are countless. The pain was manageable, and I still fought with all the energy in my bones. And now, this pain, it is so different. A mental anguish that won't be forgotten.

I go to her side, helping her out of the covers, and touching her hair affectionately.

"I hope you slept well, my sweet female, but we must be going now." I explain, motioning to our things strewn about. She nods in understanding, always so smart despite our ever-frustrating language barrier.

Elodie tries to help, but I don't let her, grabbing everything that she tries to reach for before she can.

She laughs at me, but doesn't fight, she eventually gives up. I resist a grin. My grin disintegrates before it can appear. I won't ever see this perfect creature again.

It's a sobering thought, and I hate it. But, this is the way things are, the way things have to be.

I shove items in my bag, eyeing Elodie cautiously as she pets Salsh. The rasler glances at me, pushing his big head under her hand, he rumbles contently, always enjoying her petting.

Despite how much I try to draw it out, I'm finished packing my few belongings quickly. I dread leaving, I dread taking her to where I have to leave her, but it's for the best.

Then why does my heart reject it entirely? Why do I ache? A Gladiator is taught to abandon all feelings completely, but I cannot pretend I do not feel things for Elodie.

I feel so many new things that I'm losing track.

I notice that there is a chill in the air still, even as the sun rises higher. So, I grab my cloak, and I motion for the human to stand and come forward. She obeys, always smiling at me and ready to follow what I ask. I purse my lips, going onto one knee to pull the cloak onto her slight figure. Her face flushes, and she pulls the cloak closer.

"I thght yuwer asckin meetooo marrriyu." She muses, her voice breathless. I find myself wishing for the millionth time that I could understand the words she says.

Especially now, right before saying goodbye. One conversation would be comforting. I suppose it is too much to ask.

I remain on my knee, just staring at her, trying to memorize her dark green eyes and plush lips that always turn up at the corners. I'm interrupted when Salsh comes up and begins licking Elodies face, she shrieks with laughter, the most precious sound I've had the pleasure of hearing. I smile, patting my pet on the head as sadness creeps in to dampen my mood. He would miss her almost as much as me it would seem.

Standing to my full height, I put a hand on her head and lead her in front of me, in the direction of the palace. She trustingly takes my hand, her fingers so tiny and warm. I squeeze them lightly, looking ahead only out of fear of what her face might do to me again.

We walk for a while, getting closer and closer. Elodie talks every now and then, filling the air with her soft tones to pass the time. I don't understand a word of it, but it's pleasing to my ears.

When I spot the gates to the kingdom ahead, I stop, tugging on Elodie's arm as she tries to go forward. She turns, red eyebrows raised. I simply pull her cloak hood over her head.

Walking up to the palace is one thing, but if any locals in the kingdom spot a female, we will never be able to make it without being stopped a million times by curious males.

For extra protection, I pull Elodie under my arm, draping it over her shoulder and tugging her into my chest as I keep walking. If she blends in with me, then she won't be recognized for what she really is. I'm hoping that the citizens will assume she is a smaller male.

"yur waaytoo heevyy, Barre." She grumbles at me, wiggling in my grip, I hold her firmly, not letting her escape. Her attempt is in vain. I hardly notice her struggle. She's so weak and helpless, it's amusing often times, but another reminder that she needs to be kept safe.

A forest is no place for a female, and a scarred Gladiator would not make a good mate.

After Elodie quiets down, we make our way through the palace town. The market isn't very busy, and I thank the Gods. The males hardly give us any looks, and the ones I do receive are strictly directed at me. I rarely visit the palace, and when I do, people gossip.

The sooner I get out of here, the better, I convince myself. As soon as Elodie is safe in the palace, then I can leave.

Walking down a few streets, I almost stumble when I see a few posters with big words printed on the top.

"MISSING HUMAN FEMALE: REWARD FOR SAFE RETURN"

The signs are everywhere. I was correct, they were looking for her. I am not surprised. Females are the most sought after thing on Rytaria, and even one going missing would be a priority. I stare at the reward amount. It is a good deal of coin, but I doubt that many are interested in prize money for returning her. Males are more likely to try to make her their mate.

My jaw automatically clenches at the thought. I can't help looking down at the magnificent, small thing tucked under my arm like a child. She looks around curiously, her red hair hidden in the cloak.

I have no doubt that males will fall over themselves trying to become her mate. There are many males in the palace that are more worthy of her than I am.

Elodie glances around uneasily, shrinking into me for protection.

We're getting closer and closer to the palace. I spot the guards standing at the front doors, their hands going to their hips where their blasters are holstered. I turn to Salsh, telling him to stay put. He sits on his backside, staring at me and then Elodie. I shake my head once.

"Brother, what business have you here?" One asks, stepping forward. I continue walking towards them, and even as I near they don't notice the precious treasure I have. He doesn't even glance at Elodie, that is until I pull the hood down to reveal her feminine features.

The males gasp, and I cringe when Elodie backs away from them, trying to hide in my arms. Does she not realize that this is where she belongs? In the lap of luxury, being pampered like a Goddess and showered in jewels and gifts?

She can have anything she desires here, and I'm the only thing stopping her.

"You took the female?" The other male demands, stepping forward angrily. I growl at him, furious when I see how frightened he's making Elodie.

She is trapped between 3 Rytarians that tower over her. His yelling is not helping anything, especially when she doesn't understand our language.

"I did not take her, I found her. She was alone in the great woods, afraid and injured. I saved her." I amend, and they fall silent after that. The males exchange a look, glancing at me with curiosity.

"How much do you want in reward for her?" The first one asks, and I grunt.

There is no amount of treasure in the world that compares to the value of what I really want.

Elodie stands with her head pressed into my stomach as if that will hide her from the truth. I hold her shoulders gently in my hands, trying to reassure her.

"All I ask is that she is safe and looked after. This is all I desire in exchange." I explain, and they have the nerve to look perplexed.

I forget about them for a moment, turning my full, undivided attention to Elodie. I feel like I can't breathe while I pull her away from my side by force.

She reluctantly turns her head up at me. I stare into her big green eyes, eyes that usually hold so much trust, but now they're unsure and afraid. I gently rub her upper arm. I think of all the time we have spent together. The long, warm nights spent curled into each other. The way she would sing to me while she ran her nimble fingers through my hair. Her soft, musical words that she gifted me. Her smiles. Her laughter. Her clumsy nature.

I'll miss it all. I'm too tempted to keep her, but my cute little Elodie will be better off without me.

"I... I care deeply for you, and I want you to be happy. It is the one thing I desire most." I rumble, my voice all the sudden getting too thick to speak.

She has a perplexed look on her face, and she reaches up, standing on the tips of her toes, trying to reach my neck. She doesn't succeed, she's too short. I bend at the knee and the waist, getting closer to her, until she pushes her lips against mine.

The shock of it has me stumbling back. The action disconnects our lips as my spine straightens. A growl of want springs from the depths of my throat. My eyes close briefly, enjoying the sensation of the kiss that will likely be our last.

I want to snarl as I shake my head. There is no chance of her sneaking an attack on my lips now. I stare down at her.

My hand automatically goes up to palm her face. Looking into her lush, pink face has me questioning everything. I want to kiss her. I want to nestle her in my arms every night, to tuck my head into her hair as she sings lullabies that push away the nightmares.

But I cannot. I love her, and so I must allow her to have a future where she will be happy. Happiness would not come from a life with me.

"I am sorry. I must go." I murmur, confusion blossoms on her face as I take a step back. She attempts to follow me.

"No." I say finally, my voice commanding. Elodie flinches at my harshness. "You stay here."

The female grows tears in her eyes. I press my lips together firmly to keep from going to her and stealing her away from this place.

One of the guards takes her arm in his hand. The sight grates on my temper, but I refrain from taking action.

"waree yu goin?" She wonders, but I do not even attempt to respond.

I turn around and walk away, knowing it is the best thing to do. I don't look back. Not when Salsh whines at me. Not when a tear slips down my cheek. Not even when Elodie calls out my name. I just keep walking.

Chapter 16

Elodie

My whole body trembles, fear and confusion blistering inside of me. I sniffle. I sob. My eyes leak furiously. I can't keep the emotions in to save my life.

I tried to follow after him, tried to break free from the guards holding me as Barre and Salsh walked away from me.

He left me here. He didn't even look back as I called his name.

I'm in hysterics. I can't breathe as they usher me into the palace, trying to hush me as the sobs become too much. I put my head in my hands, trying to conceal the sound of my cries. I just want Barre. I don't want to be here.

"Res ta Fray lesa relinka cru sablas." One of guards says loudly, and I attempt push them away as they crowd me.

They're so tall and broad and overwhelming. I just want Barre and his comfort and warmth. They're touching me, trying to console me.

"He... he... he left me. Why would he leave me?" I beg, gasping for air as I try to talk through my tears. They pull me, practically dragging me through the hallways.

"Please. You can't... he's coming back. He has to come back for me." I insist, wiping my tears as I fight off the male Rytarians trying to pull me deeper into the palace. I shove at their stupid shoulders, their eyes glowing down at me.

I glare up at them as I hiccup, tears constantly streaming down my face. I try to break free, wanting the taste of fresh air once again. I want to be with Barre. There's no one else as safe, as warm. I claw at the guards, trying to get them away from me so I can make a break for it.

"Barre!" I yell, but no one lets me out of the circle of people. I sob, pushing a at their arms and chests and getting nowhere. "Please."

"Relinkas! Shebassa yeltra me." One says, they all look panicked through my blurry tears.

The unbearable pain in my heart makes me stagger. I fall to the ground, my knees buckling underneath me.

No one stops me from falling, they let it happen.

"Be sey, Fray" I recognize my friend's mate's name, and I wonder if they're going to get him.

"I don't want Fray! I want Barre!" I yell, putting my face in my hands.

No one can help me, but they start to pick me up by the elbows. I scream and flail as someone effortlessly carries me away from the floor. I try to curl up in a ball, but it doesn't do anything to hinder the male holding me.

I look at the ceiling, sorrow coursing through me. I just want to be let go, I want to go back to my mate. I'm convinced that we're meant to be together. I won't let him go.

But what if he doesn't want me? Just like everyone else?

The thought has my lungs constricting like a vise is being tied around my rib cage.

He left. He left me here. There has to be a reason. Why would he just abandon me here after everything he's done for me? It doesn't add up. I don't understand. I just want him back.

I start to fight again, kicking out my legs as hard as I can. The hands on me remain firm, but as I scream a sudden shift in motion occurs. Yells ensue as the sound of a punch being landed hits my ears. Someone grabs me roughly as another Rytarian falls to the ground.

I wipe my tears away to see who is holding me like an infant, but the hands are a little too rough. A familiar sense of dread comes over me when the smell hits me. I know that smell. I know this male.

Locanas. He has me, and he's running. The speed and motion make me sick. The fight inside leaves me momentarily as fear takes over, I feel completely boneless as a sob breaks free of me. I have to fight. I can't let him terrify me again.

I kick and scream, determined to fight until the end, if that's what this is. Instead of being heard, a heavy hand clamps over my mouth to keep me quiet. I chomp down on his palm, biting into his flesh. He yells out in surprised pain, but moves his hand under my face to clamp my jaw shut.

Frustration and desperation build, and I buck and flail, trying anything to be freed from this monster. Tears blind me as I realize there's nothing I can do.

I just have to pray that Barre will come back.

Chapter 17

Barre

I stare forward as I walk, unable to look anywhere else without fear of running back and snatching Elodie up.

Salsh constantly whines next to me, glancing back anxiously at the palace as he trots slowly. He doesn't want to leave her. Neither do I.

Many stop to watch me walk by, some pointing and whispering at the last gladiator. My name is legend, my strength notorious. I'm usually bothered by those states and murmured rumors. I don't care now. Let them watch me, let them talk. Everything is pointless without her.

Though I know that she'll be better off here where she can be cared for, leaving just feels wrong.

I clench my fists at my sides, picturing running my fingers through her hair. The recollection of tracing her brown speckle covered skin makes it hard to breathe.

How did this happen? How do I hold so much love in my heart for her when I've only know pain and violence?

I glance up just in time to see that I'm at the front gates. The woods lay ahead, a whole different world from this place, a world I prefer.

The cobblestones beneath my boots cut off abruptly, turning into dirt ahead. I stop where I stand, exactly one step away from encountering the wilderness, where I belong.

For the first time since leaving Elodie at the palace, I turn back to stare at the building's grandeur. That's where she belongs... right?

I run a hand over my hair, pulling at the strands and hating this back and forth inside me. I want to believe I could be enough for that precious female, but I don't feel adequate. Someone so unbelievably important and beautiful wouldn't want to be with me.

But what if she does?

A pang of longing and hope flares to life inside my chest. A sudden magnetism erupts, and it seems to be pulling me back to where she is, away from my den. That cabin is no longer my home, because Elodie is the only sanctuary I need.

Maybe she will want to stay in the palace, but I have to try at the very least. This could be my one shot at happiness. I have to try.

I think of all the times she touched me, smiled at me, that affection couldn't be made up by my imagination.

With my mind made up, I turn on my heel and begin marching back up the streets of the Capital. I have to get back to tell her how I feel. We could get translation devices, and then no words would be left unsaid.

The city is buzzing with life, and I ignore it all as Salsh trots alongside me. He has a spring in his step, excited to be going back for the female that touched our lives. I share a soft smile with him, equally excited, but filled with nerves.

I have to see her, I have to try.

I swiftly make my way back to the front doors of the palace. I halt, realizing that the doors are wide open, and the guards are gone, along with my heart.

Where is Elodie?

I push past the doors, ignoring the towering marble pillars and ornate, ancient paintings lining the walls. None of it matters.

My heart stops as I see guards running in every direction, panicked looks exchanged between Rytarians, harsh frantic words spilling from trembling mouths.

I see one of the guards I handed Elodie off to. I charge towards him, grabbing him by his armor and lifting him off the ground so I can look him in the eyes. His pupils are muddied with fear.

"Where is she? Where did she go?" I demand, my heart thudding erratically, the sound thundering in my ears insistently.

"She's gone. Someone attacked me, and took her. We can't find her anywhere." He insists, grabbing on my wrists and trying to pull them away from him, a pathetic attempt as my fists tighten.

A familiar heat spreads through my limbs, the same feeling that assailed me in the ring when I was a gladiator.

The urge to wreak havoc.

Chapter 18

Barre

Anger pulses through me, and any control I had left is wilting away. I'm going insane.

"What do you mean? Where did she go? She was just here!" I demand, still gripping the guard with tight, desperate hands. I saw Elodie moments ago. I wasn't even in the woods when I turned back.

The sinking feeling in my gut worsens.

I can feel my heart thumping wildly in my chest, panic surging. Where could she have gone? Why do I have such a bad feeling about this?

"Fray, Fray, thank the Gods that you're here!" The Rytarian in my hands wheezes the words out, I whirl around to see General Fray walking quickly to us.

I let go of the guard, he stumbles to the ground. I'm ready to go to war. Fray's yellow eyes widen when I get in his face.

"Where is she? Where is my Elodie?" I rage, seeing nothing but red. Salsh growls next to me, taking a threatening step forward as he bares his teeth.

"You're the one that brought her back? She's been with you all this time?" He wonders, obviously perplexed. I growl. There is no time for these questions when my precious female is missing.

"Has she been taken? Where is she?" I demand, and Fray holds up his hands.

It's the first time I notice the female behind him.

She has tears running down her face.

"Elodie? ware ees Elodie?" She asks, and Fray shushes her.

"We will find her, my mate, I told you to stay put. Your worrying is not good for our kit."

"Tell me where she is, Fray, or I swear to the Gods I will tear this palace down to find her!" I growl, not caring when the guards jump away from me, or when Fray's mate breaks out into sobs. The little human pushes her face into the General's chest, crying.

Fray glares at me for upsetting his mate. All I can seem to care about is finding the one female I care about more than this whole planet.

"There is a warrior here, he has become obsessed with Elodie. I don't doubt that he would be the one that took her." Fray says, holding his human mate to his chest as she continues to cry.

I growl furiously, my arms straightening as I flex.

"What is his name?"

I need to know the name of the male I am going to kill.

"Locanas."

Everything quickly falls into place, and I realize this is the reason she's always been afraid. Always looking over her shoulder, trembling at sudden noises. My Elodie was terrified of this Locanas person, he even haunted her dreams.

I will make him pay with his blood.

"Where could they be? Where would he have taken her?" I don't even try to keep my voice down.

The little human female sniffles, turning her head to look up at me.

"I dddone-t no." She whines, and I raise my eyebrows.

Fray is watching me.

"You can't understand her? You don't have a transaction chip?"

I shake my head once. All of this is a waste of time to me. If I don't find Elodie now, I will kill someone or destroy something. The anger inside me pulses with its own life. I can't hardly think straight. I see red, transported to my days of fighting and killing.

"Let's go. We will find Locanas, and get you a translator in the process. That will make everything easier I think."

I glare, following him down the hallway quickly. One of the guards tries to tell me that no raslers are allowed here, but one bark from Salsh has him shutting his mouth.

I should never have taken Elodie here. She was afraid, she was always afraid, and I never knew why until now. It's all my fault. I should've personally escorted her to the Emperor. Instead, I let her be in danger.

How can I ever forgive myself?

We file into some sort of room where many Rytarian males are gathered. Fray goes through another door, quickly coming out with a translation chip in hand. I don't waste time shoving the thing in my ear. The pain is temporary. I turn to Fray's mate, ready to interrogate her.

"Where is my female?" I ask, clenching my fists at my side. I won't rest until she's found.

"Like I said, I don't know. I heard she was returned, but when we got to the Guards, it was too late. I know it was him. It has to be that big bastard." She sobs, clutching a tissue to her face as her crying takes over.

"Where would he take her? What does he want from her?" I demand answers.

A young warrior steps forward.

"He spoke often of her, he wants her for his mate."

Fray growls low.

"I thought he was over that. I told him he wasn't allowed to court her."

I pale.

"So he plans to mate her by force then?" I ask, fear penetrating my heart. No one answers me. That's the only answer I need. My worst fears are coming true.

We need to find her. Now.

"We'll split up. Look anywhere and everywhere. He can't have gotten far with her. Report back to Barre. He'll take care of Locanas, I'm sure." Fray looks to me for confirmation. I nod. I will likely kill the male that dared to terrify one as pure and sweet as my Elodie.

Praying to the Gods that I'm not too late, I hurry to find her before anything bad can happen to her.

I turn, stomping through the hallway quickly. All the males split up in different directions. Finding my female is their priority now.

I try any door that I can, not finding anything but furniture and large rooms. Around me the halls are filled with Rytarians searching for the lost treasure that is Elodie. I have to find her before something happens. The terror coursing through me is enough to halt my breathing.

How am I supposed to find her when the thought along of her pain and fear makes me weak at the knees?

Salsh suddenly darts in front of me, his nose twitching. And that's when I realize that I had him here all along. A hunting rasler's sense of smell is unmatched.

I frantically search my pockets for Elodie's hair ribbon, going to my knee to show it to him. Slash stares at the ribbon, pressing his nose to the fabric and taking a long whiff of it.

His red eyes dart up to my face to meet my gaze.

"Find her."

And he's off. I run after my pet as he sprints down the long hallways, passing every corridor and door. His snout is high in the air, searching for any faint whiff of her that he can find.

He leads me through a hall that takes us to the kitchens. I narrow my eyes at our surroundings. Could Salsh have made a mistake? Did he follow his nose to food?

The rasler jumps over the counters, sending pots and pans clattering to the ground. He runs further into the heart of the kitchens. I chase after him.

I follow him into a dark alleyway, realizing that my companion has stopped at a wooden door. He claws at the door, snarling and foaming at the mouth.

That's when I hear it. Crying.

I pull Slash away, trying the doorknob and finding it locked. I growl, throwing my shoulder into the solid door. It gives way the first try, sending me tripping into a small pantry.

A male turns his head, his eyes wide with surprise, and panic. He's kneeling on the ground.

"It can't be." He says. "Gladiator."

I barrel into the room, grabbing him and pulling until I see what his body is hiding. Elodie lays sprawled out on the floor. She's trembling, her eyes puffy from crying, her cheeks wet with tears. A sob leaves her. My heart ripples in my chest.

Her body, her delicate, soft body is exposed. Her bright pink, round teats are visible, her shirt torn into tatters by desperate male hands.

It's then and there that I decide I will end him now.

I drag Locanas into the alley and away from my female.

I don't think, I don't hesitate, I just attack.

Pinning him to the ground like he easily did to a helpless female, I lay my fists into his face. Over and over and over.

Blood sprays my face, and I don't stop for anything. Not the hands clawing at my back, not the shouts around me, I won't stop, I will kill him. His life is mine to take away. I'm transported back to my days in the arena. It was so easy to kill back then, it's easier now that my purpose has arrived.

Elodie is that purpose.

The male struggles, his arms pushing at me. He's strong, but I'm stronger. I put my hand around his neck, slamming the back of his skull into the ground again and again until he stops fighting me.

I could kill him easily now, a few more hits, a snap of his neck, he would be dead in moments. I could sink my thumbs into his eyes for daring to look at flesh as heavenly as her's. I could crush his windpipe for breathing on her beautiful face. I could crack each of his fingers one by one for daring to traumatize her with his touch.

It's one word that stops me. A broken, little voice calling my name.

"Barre."

I pause over the bloody mess that is Locanas's face. My jaw clenched, my breath coming in and out of my lungs.

"Barre. Where is he? Please."

I look over my shoulder to see Elodie. She's surrounded by males, and Fray's mate is there too, pulling Elodie's torn shirt to cover her chest.

My eyes lock with the tiny she. Her green eyes still shimmer with tears.

I wonder how I must look to her now. Painted in blood, eyes wild with fury. I'm deadly. I'm a destroyer of life. I hate to think of her fear now being directed at me.

I stand, leaving Locanas. It's hard to do. I want to finish the job, but I can't bring myself to kill in front of such innocent eyes.

The sea of males parts for me. I'm much stronger than them all, and they know it. They won't get in my way after the dominance I just displayed.

My fists are soaked in purple, Locanas's blood is everywhere. These males fear me, but the only person I have eyes for is Elodie.

I pause, standing above her, going to my knees until I'm on her level.

I open my mouth to say something, to say anything really. I'm reminded of the day I found her trembling and crying in the woods. I tentatively reach for her, unsure of what to do. Before I can say a word, she throws her arms around me. I catch her, my mouth hanging open in surprise.

She sobs, clinging to my neck.

"I knew you would come back."

Chapter 19

Elodie

I can hardly see through the throng of tears flooding my eyes. The warmth of Barre's chest and the comfort of Soleil's words are my only security from the trauma threatening to suffocate me.

"Elodie, oh my gosh, are you okay?" My best friend demands, trying to pry at Barre's arms to get to me. He doesn't budge, instead he just glares at her. He hands grip his biceps, pulling and tugging to no avail.

I sob once, glancing over at Locanas as he manages to stand up, stumbling slightly as a guard grabs him by the elbow. His eyes find mine through the small crowd of people, and I want more than anything to disappear. I can't even look away. I'm frozen. Fright has made me it's home.

Locanas is staring at me with his blood drenched face. His gaze is flooded with sorrow.

Barre forcibly turns my head to disconnect our connection, and I'm glad for it. I wrap my arms around his midsection tighter, blinking rapidly to dislodge my tears. I listen to his heart thudding evenly in his chest.

"Misha, matayunca. Frola." He murmurs to me, petting my hair with fingers that are soaked in drying purple blood, oddly enough.

He nearly killed my attacker. I don't know what to think. No one has ever done something like that for me.

I hiccup, trying my best to breathe in Barre's calming smell. I think of being curled up in his bed, safe in the little cabin in the woods. A roaring fire. A bowl of soup. No one but me and him.

I turn my face into his neck.

Something cold and wet nudges my arm, and I look up briefly to see Salsh. He licks the tears off my face before Barre pushes him away.

"Elodie, oh my gosh. What did he do to you? He didn't... he didn't..." The word rape is stuck in Soleil's throat, and I don't blame her. It's a difficult question to ask.

I shake my head adamantly.

"No he didn't rape me, but he... he did touch me." I whisper, remembering the rough hands grabbing at my breasts.

Tears sting my eyes once again as Barre growls furiously under me.

"Astasha furlenki es tunsa." He spits, his normally calm voice harsh, and Soleil's eyebrows furrow.

"What do you mean by that?" She asks him, and he responds quickly.

"Relinkas tes meneas. Elodie emsa meneas." He grouches. Soleil's mouth drops open in shock.

Confusion bubbles up inside me. He can understand her? He can understand us? I gulp, finally voicing my questions.

"He understands?" I ask, completely speechless when Barre nods. Somehow he got a translation chip while Locanas was holding me captive.

I've never known such fear in all my life. He carried me in here, held me down while he tore my shirt open. I screamed and fought and cried with all my might, but his strength was terrifying. I was completely powerless against him. I thought I was going to die.

Remembering it has me overwhelmed all over again, and my heart starts racing. Even with Barre's arms around me, terror courses through me. I start shaking, trying to make sense of it all.

"He says you're his? Have you been with him all this time?" Soleil asks gently, putting a hand on my back. I nod meekly, noticing the way Barre doesn't even look at her. He only has eyes for me as his hand gently caresses my face up and down with the back of his fingers.

Fear still has a hold on me, I can barely speak.

"Yes." I manage, glancing away from my rescuer. "I thought I was his mate, but he left me here. I'm not so sure."

He came back for me though, and told Soleil that I'm his apparently. That has to count for something.

"Misha." The endearment rolls off Barre's lips, and I turn my tear filled face to him. His mismatched eyes are so tender that my bottom lip trembles. "Shebsta les nera mes relinkas. Mesun ablant els cantrinas."

Locanas gasps, Soleil covers her mouth. I want to ask my best friend what Barre said, but as soon as I open my mouth, Fray steps forward, obvious anger on his face. I shy away, still filled with fright from the top of my head to the tips of my toes.

"Shelesna tel Locanas mesta tas empeisantra." He says, and that makes my alien react, he stands, holding me tightly bridal style. I cling to him as I'm lifted 7 feet off the ground.

"He's taking us to the Emperor to figure out what to do about Locanas." Soleil whispers, and from this height I can't even see her. I gulp, feeling embarrassed about all of this. I don't want to make so much trouble.

Knowing full well that Barre can understand me now, I turn to look up at him. All his attention remains on me.

His expression is chalk full of gentle concern, but there's a determined set to his jaw.

"Can't we just go back? To your home? I don't wanna be here anymore." I can't keep the pain out of my voice, or the tears from forming.

Barre's face hardens, and shakes his head. Disappointment blossoms in sadness.

"Mesa retreplin forsurntru can." He insists, I cringe at the harsh tone.

I turn my head in an awkward angle to peak down at Soleil, hating that she has to see me in such a mess.

"What did he say?"

Her brown eyes are wide.

"He said, 'First I'll make him pay.'." She enlightens me.

Oh.

Chapter 20

Barre

Rage is something I used to release at will. It's not something I kept inside, something I hid. Now, it is shoved down deep, locked away without a way out as I stare at the enemy walking ahead of me. He may be held captive, but I want more.

I pin Elodie to my chest, relieved that she's okay, for the most part. She did not come out of the incident completely unscathed, and for that I blame myself.

Someone handed Locanas a rag to hold to his massively bloody face. Every drop of the purple liquid spilt is more than deserved. Kindness towards him is not. He has not earned mercy.

It takes everything in me not to rush forward to finish the job of killing him. I dream of how completely easy it would be to end his existence.

We walk down the hallways of the palace, up the whirling staircases and through ornate doorways. I carry Elodie the whole way, listening to her beautiful words every step of the way.

She clutches at my clothes, murmuring to me.

"Thank you for saving me. I just knew you would come back. Please, don't leave me again." Elodie whispers, and guilt stabs my chest.

I have failed her. This is why I never should have tried to be a mate for her, I'll never be enough.

"I'm so sorry, tiny. No one will touch you again. I will try harder to be the male you need. I'm not sure if I can live without you." I touch Elodie's bright red locks, wondering how I will ever win her trust back.

Or if I even deserve it.

Elodie doesn't react to my words, still unaware of what they mean.

After some debate with Fray, we decided to leave the kitchens and bring a bloodied Locanas to the Emperor. The Emperor is the highest authority on Rytaria, and he serves justice in serious situations such as these.

And serious it is. I want a harsh punishment dealt, I will settle for nothing less. Execution or life in prison. I'll be happy with either, though death would be the more fair option. It would be even better if get to put an end to his life.

Seeing Elodie's clothes torn open like that, her tears and desperate cries... just thinking of them makes me hot with anger. I demand revenge.

I pull her up, covering my little Elodie better, hiding her from any and all eyes. Fray's mate, Soleil constantly tries to check up on my female. I realize that they are friends, but I'm still protective. Any being trying to get close to tiny has my hackles rising.

Soleil nears me, walking on her toes to try to catch a glimpse of what's mine. I grunt, lifting the little human in my arms higher. The smaller, pregnant female huffs in annoyance. Her black eyebrows furrow in frustration, and for a moment I think she's considering climbing me to get to her friend. Too bad. Elodie is mine. I've decided it.

As long as she agrees.

"Enough, my mate. Do not upset him, he is dangerous. His threat level is.." I turn my gaze to General Fray to glare at him. It's enough to shut his mouth.

I adjust Elodie's body in my arms uncomfortably as she sniffles, her green eyes on me curiously at my shift in demeanor. I'm glad for once that she can't understand the Rytarian language.

I've never been comfortable with people speaking of my threat level. I don't care for the attention.

"Here we are." Fray speaks, gesturing to the large doors with his head, holding tightly to his mate's shoulders. "Maybe you should stay out here, my heart."

His hand goes down to palm her small belly that is only just beginning to swell with a kit. A pang of envy jolts through me.

I look down at Elodie. All lush red waves, brown speckles, and smiles. I picture having a kit with her, and my heart speeds up. Just thinking of something so wonderful has me wanting, especially when I think of what we would do to create another being.

I curse myself for having such thoughts after what just happened. I am too selfish.

"Fray, I am going in there, whether you like it or not, you big bully! You can't just tell me what to do all the time." She demands, and he simply nods, as if he's entirely accustomed to the way she talks.

I raise my eyebrows in interest. Usually on Rytaria, males are considered the leaders. Since our jobs are to protect and provide for a female, the female is to listen and follow what we say, especially when it comes to their safety.

Maybe humans are different, but I cannot imagine Elodie speaking to me in such a way. She's so gentle, and keeps to herself. Soleil seems very different from my Elodie. She is fire, while my human is a flower.

"Bring his pathetic hide in, he has a lot to answer for." Fray instructs the guards, the ones dragging Locanas.

I refrain from snarling, hating to see him still alive and breathing.

We all walk into the throne room, the Emperor standing in front of us, decorated in fine jewels and silk clothing. His dark blonde hair is wild around his angular face.

"The female has been found?" He demands, striding towards me quickly, his eyes set on Elodie's unkempt red hair. I look over my shoulder, a little uneasy and annoyed. I've never had an easy time with authority. This must be done though.

My mate needs justice.

"Yes, sir. It seems the weeks she has been gone, she was with Barre. He brought her back to the palace, only for Locanas to snatch her, and..." Fray trails off, clamping a hand around the back of his mate's neck for reassurance as he looks at me.

The reminder of what the dishonorable male did to my female has me clenching my jaw. Elodie stirs, still blissfully unaware of the words being exchanged around her. I press her against my chest. She seems content to remain silent while I hold her.

"What? What did he do?" The Emperor wonders urgently. No one wants to say the words. I step forward to answer, but a flurry of motion stops me.

A female steps in from a side door, adorned in many expensive silken fabrics that hug her protruding belly. The female is surrounded by her own guards. She wears a crown on her head.

So, this is the Emperor's human mate? Is every human mate pregnant in this kingdom?

She rushes in, swift for someone who is with child.

"Well, from the looks of it, he did something unforgivable. Believe me, I should know." She stands by her mate for a moment, sharing a look with him. The Emperor's eyes go wide in understanding.

The Empress walks towards me, and everyone parts to give her access to my female and I.

I stand remarkably still as she stops, this close I can see that she's taller than my Elodie, or Fray's Soleil. Still small though.

"Does she need medical attention?" She asks in a hushed tone. Amazed at her calm demeanor, I shake my head.

"He did not rape her, but he tried." I answer, my tone brutal. If there were not two pregnant females, and I was not holding Elodie, I would be killing him here and now.

"I did not! Please." Locanas dares to beg, trying to tear himself free from the guards holding him. Blood dribbles from his face to the marble floors.

I growl, a natural reaction to the male.

"No, you do not get to speak. There is no other explanation. Her clothes are torn open. I will likely find bruises all over her for weeks to come. You have no honor." I spit, and Locanas shakes his head.

The Emperor clears his throat, and suddenly all eyes are on him.

"No matter how things appear, let the male share his side. I want all sides of the story." He insists, and I want to shout in protest, but I keep quiet.

He is the ruler here, I am no longer in the woods anymore. I have no authority here. I despise it, but there is nothing I can do.

The guards release Locanas, who stumbles forward. I hate the way he looks at the bundle of sweetness in my arms with sorrow and yearning.

"I want a mate, so very much. The first day I saw Elodie, I thought she would be perfect. I tried to court her, but she always ran away. I thought if I.. if I tried to seduce her, she would see what a good mate I could be for her. I would never rape a female. I just wanted to give her pleasure."

An involuntary snarl escapes me, Elodie flinches.

"You fool, that is rape. She did not want it, so it would be rape."

He has the nerve to look surprised.

"I did not know, I swear it. I did no more than touch her teats. I thought she would like it." His lips tighten in shame, his eyes downcast as they become shimmery with unshed tears. "I am sorry."

Everyone in the throne room is silent, but I'm still blistering with anger.

"How did you not know that you were assaulting her? How are you so ignorant?" I demand. He seems genuinely in his regret, but I do not forgive him. It's not my place to forgive him.

"I.. I do not have parents. I never have, I was left on the streets as a kit, I ate from the trash and slept in alleyways. I was alone until I trained to become a warrior. I was not taught the ways of females. I was a reject." He glances at Elodie, a muscle in his jaw ticking. "I saw a similar look in Elodie's eyes. I thought she would understand me. I thought I wouldn't be alone anymore. I want a mate. I want kits of my own. I don't want to be alone anymore."

Glaring, I shake my head, especially when I see the empathy he receives. No one is angry anymore. I don't believe it.

I take a threatening stomp towards Locanas. His excuses are not enough.

"Wanting a mate does not make you unique. I wish for one as well, as do many males. That doesn't mean you can torture a female. You should have patiently waited, instead you tortured a helpless Goddess. Shame on you."

Locanas hangs his head, and Elodie clutches at my shirt, like she knows the weight of my words.

The room is remarkably quiet, the Emperor strides forward. He stands by his mate, taking her hands in his own.

"Obviously Locanas needs to face consequences for his actions, but I believe with some learning he could be an honorable male. Although, Locanas, you will need thorough evaluation before you can be around a female, let alone have a mate. I believe redemption is possible for you. You seem to have good intentions, and I believe your heart is true."

Outrage courses through me, and it takes everything in me not to go into an uncontrollable rage.

"No. He should be thrown into the dungeons. Executed. Exiled. Anything to pay for his crimes." I insist loudly, tightening my hold on little Elodie and thanking the Gods she does not understand the debate going on.

Fray clears his throat. I snap my gaze onto him in an instant.

"You have no authority here, Barre, I'm sorry."

I growl, frustrated.

"I want to be her mate, if she'll have me. That gives me enough authority to insist he gets a much worse punishment. He hurt her. I won't stand for it." The anger inside me is building, demanding to be let out in the form of violence.

I'm transported back to my days in the gladiator ring, weapons tethered to my hips and a sword in my hand. I killed many. Gladiators were only allowed to fight high treason criminals. I never lost. I took all my frustrations out on those criminals. I stole their lives.

What I wouldn't give to be back in the arena with Locanas across from me. I would destroy him, annihilate his existence, erase his soul from this planet. Nothing would give me more satisfaction.

I can't, and I hate it.

"Something can be said for the fact that he didn't know how truly delicate these humans are. Their weakness, it is obvious enough, but not many know the extent of their fragility." The Emperor states, arms raised to garner attention, as if his authoritative voice wasn't enough.

Confusion blossoms in my chest. What?

"What do you mean?" Locanas demands, and I narrow my eyes at him, wishing he didn't voice my own question before I got the chance to ask it.

The Empress wears a small smile.

"I'm sure you're aware of threat level, yes?" She poses the question at me, not daring a glance at Locanas.

I nod, slightly embarrassed. I suppose news of my infamous strength has spread to these new females. I have a threat level of 154, the highest on the planet.

It's not something I enjoy boasting about.

"Well. Human females aren't exactly... gifted.. in that area." She says.

My face must display my confusion, because the Emperor is quick to explain.

"They only hold a threat level 1. Each one we've tested. Only a level 1. They are very delicate."

I can't hide my shock. My hold on Elodie automatically loosens. A 1? How can that be? I never would've guessed. I knew my precious female was weak, but I had no idea how far off I was. It's shocking.

"I did not know. There is so much I do not know about females. Please, I know I deserve to be punished. I'm sorry. I want to learn." Locanas is determined to have his voice heard.

The menace takes a few steps towards me, his eyes set on Elodie as if he can apologize to her. Before I can tell him off, a snarl erupts as Salsh steps in front of us, showing Locanas his teeth.

"Step away." I insist, watching as Elodie burrows her face into my neck and trembles. She squeezes her eyes shut.

"Please." She murmurs. My heart breaks.

"Just get him out of here. Let me take her away. She needs rest."

"Yes of course. Lead Locanas to the dungeons while we decide what to do with him. I'm sure him being secured will put Elodie at ease." The Emperor commands, and guards rush forward to fulfil his command.

Locanas doesn't struggle, because he knows he deserves to be locked away. I relax slightly as soon as he's marched out of the throne room. Elodie will feel safer now that he's gone.

I glance around, waiting impatiently for someone to give us a place to let my human relax. I turn to her, brushing her hair with my fingertips. I cup the back of her head, her face pressed into my neck. I wish I could take away her pain.

There's a flourish of activity as the Emperor approaches me with his mate. I cautiously take a step back.

"Please, Gladiator, we just want to help. Fray." The Emperor raises a hand, beckoning the General forward. He strides slowly towards us, his hand on his mate's back.

"Take Barre and his..." He trails off, not sure what label to give Elodie. "Human to an empty den. They need time to themselves."

I turn, about to follow Fray, when Elodie speaks up. I stop in my tracks.

"Wait." She murmurs, looking up into my eyes. Being able to hear her, truly hear her, is amazing. "I want to say something, to the Emperor and his mate. Please."

I turn around once more, giving her what she wants.

Our leader steps forward to hear what she has to say.

"Thank you."

It's a small gesture, but not one I will soon forget. She has sweet manners.

The Empress takes Elodie's hands in hers, smiling sweetly.

"Of course, and if you ever need anything, ask for me personally."

I carry her away after that, walking through the great halls and feeling misplaced. The only thing in this whole palace that makes me feel welcome is Elodie.

She fills all the lonely spots in my heart, she makes me whole. When I bury my face in her hair, smelling the red locks, and wondering why I ever thought I could leave her here.

It was fate that brought her onto my lands. Finding her wasn't an accident, I know that now. I was meant for her, and she for me. Thinking of losing her, or harm coming to her, it pains me. I don't want to go back to my old life before her. I can't.

Now that I've experienced heaven, I don't want to give it up.

Chapter 21

Barre

When the door closes behind us, Fray and Soleil disappear. The pregnant human was reluctant to leave her friend's side. They have a connection I'll never quite understand. Eventually, she realized that we need privacy now.

The General is off to go find a translation chip for Elodie. It will be a relief for her to finally understand me. Just as I was ecstatic to hear her words clearly after all this time. It's a miracle. It's something I need to focus on right now.

I'm still bristling with anger. Not only at Locanas, but the Emperor for not allowing me to execute the rapist on the spot.

I command Slash to lay down by the door, still paranoid in this unfamiliar place. I carry Elodie through the roomy den and to the nest in the corner of the room.

This place is so unlike my own den. Everything is sleek and expensive.

Now Elodie can get a full look at what she would be missing if she went back to my den with me.

It astonished me when she asked me if we could go back. It's all I can think of as I lay her down on the nest, the covers made of the finest silken materials the palace can offer.

I guess it just proves that she cares for me, to give all of this up to come be with me. Does that mean she wants to be my mate?

The thought is sweet poison, it wants to take me over, but I push it away. Now is not the time. I must comfort my Elodie, whatever she is to me, she's important.

As soon as I climb over her in the nest, she reaches her slim arms for me, her soft skiing sliding across my neck as she clings to my body. She's still shaking, and my jaw clenches as pain sprouts in my chest. I should've been there. I should go back and kill Locanas, no matter what the Emperor says.

"He will pay. I will make sure of it." I vow, laying down with Elodie as she clings to me, whimpering low when I let go of her for even a split second. It seems she's traumatized, all because of that bastard.

I don't care for his ridiculous excuses. Sure, they explain his insolence, but how could he not know he was hurting her? Humans are obviously small and powerless against us. If it was a female Rytarian he was trying to rape, he would be put in his place. But, my poor Elodie could not put up a fight. I clench my fists at the idea.

She was helpless against him. She likely fought for all she was worth, all her strength used just to be overpowered. The idea of such a feeling makes me sick. Her fear is not unwarranted.

I lean against the back of the wall, pulling her to me and tucking her into my arms, telling her that she's safe with my body language.

Elodie's trembling subsides, her tears dry and her breathing evens. She pulls back slightly, looking up at me with shining green eyes. I gulp. I want her to speak. I need more of her beautiful words.

"I love you."

And that's when my heart triples in speed. This magnificent creature loves me. Me. A beast. A Heathen. A monster. How am I worthy of the love of someone so pure?

"I would die for you. You mean more to me than... than anything I've ever loved." I murmur, fully aware that the words mean nothing until a tiny translation device buries into her ear. I brush my fingers across her cheek to try to convey my message as best I can.

She turns, staring up at me with glimmering green eyes.

"You... you love me too?" Elodie wonders out loud.

I nod slowly, smiling when her face flashes red. I adore when her odd human ways show. I remember the first time I saw that red fill her little face. It fascinated me.

Elodie grips me with as much strength as she has left in her trembling body when a knock reverberates through the room.

Salsh jumps up, a fierce growl on his lips.

"Come in." I say, and Fray's face appears, he glances at Slash who is still growling fiercely. He's on edge, we all are.

"I have the translation chip." He holds up a sleek case to show me, Elodie nestles closer to me, averting her eyes as spasms wrack her delicate spine. "Should I bring it in?"

I shake my head once.

"She is too afraid. Put it on the ground and leave."

Fray nods in understanding, slowly lowering the case to the ground, watching Salsh all the while. Finally the General leaves quietly, and it's as if he was never here.

I make a click with my mouth, and the rasler jumps to attention.

"Retrieve." I command, glancing at the case to lock his target. He immediately grabs it in his mouth, carrying it eagerly to my side and placing it on the nest.

I suddenly wish I had a treat to reward him.

Shifting my precious arm full of soft female, I lift the case in my fingers, my hand flexing and jaw clenching as I realize what I must do. What has to be done in order to ensure our communication is not going to be easy. A small hand reaches into my line of sight, grabbing my wrist gently to gain my attention.

"I know it'll hurt. I don't care. Nothing is worse than not being able to understand you." The dried tear trails on her face make my chest clench, how can I let more pain come to her when she's been through enough today?

Elodie sighs, grabbing for the case with a speed that I wasn't expecting. She tries to pry it from my hands, but my grip is much stronger than hers.

She is a threat level 1. That's a fact that I still can't quite grasp.

"Okay, fine." I relent, disgruntled that she wants me to hurt her. I suppose it's a necessary hurt, and it'll happen at some point anyway.

I click the case open, grabbing the little device and turning to Elodie with a glare. She shys away from me, and the slight hesitation on her face hurts. I close my eyes, gathering myself with a deep breath. I try to give her a convincing smile to win back her favor.

It works, and she relaxes against me while I bring the translator to her ear. I cup her head in my other hand, keeping her as still as possible and comforting her with a brush of my thumb across her cheekbone.

The translation chip attacks, burrowing into her ear without warning. Suddenly, she stiffens, but doesn't make a sound as pain flashes across her face. The amount of pride I feel in her for being brave is astonishing. I squeeze her tight as the agony passes.

Her brilliant green eyes blink open. Anticipation glimmers in her gaze.

"Say something." She commands breathlessly.

"I love you."

Elodie's eyes fill with tears, and she grabs my neck.

"Really?" She wonders, and I nod, amused and annoyed at her for questioning me.

"Yes. You have become everything to me. I have never felt so much love for someone." I murmur, unable to stop myself from touching her.

She smiles broadly, displaying her white teeth before it disappears. Doubt resurfaces.

"Then why did you try to leave me here?" Elodie wonders. I feel so much guilt for even trying to leave her, knowing what I do now, knowing that she loves me.

"Because I thought... I know that it's what's best for you. You are a female, but not only that, you are the most precious being I've ever encountered. How can I even begin to try to provide you with the luxury you deserve, tiny?"

Her face furrows.

"Tiny?" She asks, and I smile gently.

"That's what I have been calling you."

"So that's what misha means." She sounds oddly upset about this.

I chuckle, playing with a lock of her hair. I spin the curl around my finger.

"What did you think it meant?" I wonder, and her face turns bright red again. I touch her cheeks where the color lies. "This is lovely."

Somehow, the red deepens a shade at my words. She pushes my hand away. I narrow my eyes, wishing to touch her, but respecting her boundaries.

"I don't know. My love, something romantic like that." She shrugs, putting her palms on her face to cover her beautiful oddity from my gaze.

I lean towards her, our breath mingling as I lower my face towards hers.

"Would you like it if I called you my love?" I ask, and her breath catches, suddenly she's pulling the blanket closer to her chest.

She won't look at me.

"Maybe." She responds, glancing at me through her lashes. "But Barre, how could you think that? How could you think that I would prefer a rich and spoiled life? Do I seem that shallow?"

I shake my head.

"No, no, never that. I just think you deserve the best. A life with me.. it wouldn't be easy. I didn't want to ask it of you. That would be asking you to give up being pampered and waited on like the Goddess you are."

We're both silent for a long moment, and then she laughs.

"What's so amusing, little human?"

She straightens, propping herself up on her elbow.

"So, everything you did for me, you don't think that was enough?" She presses, I open my mouth to respond, but she keeps talking. "You treated me like a Queen in your house. You fed me and built fires to keep me warm, you comforted me when I was terrified, you watched over me. You protected me. You dressed my wounds and... and..." Elodie tries to catch her breath after talking as fast as she can. She practically spit the words at me.

It takes a moment to process what she's saying.

"You think that's enough?" I ask, and since she's still panting she simply nods.

"It's" she breathes, "more than" breath "enough."

It's my turn to be confused. Although, I suppose Elodie is different in many ways to the female Rytarians who once walked the planet. She doesn't ask for fine jewels or silk sheets. She doesn't demand the best of everything. She wants me.

"Praise the gods." I reach for her, but stop myself.

Elodie's red eyebrows quirk.

"What? What's wrong?" I purse my lips, my body thrumming with physical awareness. Every part of me wants her.

"I don't... I can't touch you. I don't want to overwhelm you after..."

"Locanas." She finishes in a whisper. I nod, looking away from her pale, brown flecked shoulder. Seeing it exposed is somehow erotic, but I can control myself. It is why I am an infamous Gladiator. Control is key in every element of my life. This is no exception.

Elodie seems to ponder this for a while, biting her lip in a way that tempts me to devour her whole.

"Can I ask you something?"

"Anything." I respond, knowing that conversation is a welcomed distraction I need right now.

"Do you want me as your mate? Like, do you plan on making me yours? You'll take me back to your cabin and things will go back to how they were before you brought me here?"

Is that even a question?

"Yes. I wouldn't have it any other way. Unless you choose otherwise. But I want you. I need you in a way I don't understand, Elodie."

"Good answer." She responds. "I want to try something."

She's grabbing my hand then, lifting it as she shifts her body in such a way that causes the blanket to fall away. My eyes widen and I scramble to sit up as she drags my hand to her exposed teats.

I hold my breath as my heart beats erratically in my chest. She presses my hand to her breast, the pale flesh is tender and heavenly to the touch. I'm frozen briefly as it fills my hand completely, and then I give a gentle squeeze. The ball of soft fat gives way under my hungry fingers. I groan when she arches into me, a slight whimper leaving her.

My control snaps for the second time today, and I'm kissing her like my survival depends on it. Her tongue delves into my mouth, and I enjoy every second of it. Our hot breath mingles, my body is alive with electricity and so much love I can hardly breathe.

I take my lips off of hers, latching onto her neck instead as I greedily continue to knead her flesh in my palm. I'm tempted to take her right here and now.

"You're nothing like him." The whisper in my ear catches me off guard. I pull away slightly, her burning gaze startles me. "I need your touch. I'm yours. He wanted to take what wasn't his, what I wasn't willing to give him. It's all yours because I say so."

The reminder of Locanas and what he did instantly changes my mood. It steals my arousal and leaves fury in its place.

"He deserves death." I say, making Elodie pale.

"What are they going to do with him?" She wonders. I have to take my hand away from her teat before I clench my hands into fists.

I wish I could tell her that he's to be executed, or that he'll spend the rest of his miserable life in prison. I can't. I hate it. I feel like I've let her down in a major way for not making him pay.

"I don't know yet. They're deciding." I keep my voice calm for Elodie's sake. I can't shove aside the guilt assaulting me.

She's asked me to be her mate, which I happily accept, but I can't even bring her justice. I'm already proving to be a lousy mate.

"Oh." She murmurs, and I can hear the pain and confusion in her little voice. I want to comfort her with words, but I decide enough has been said already, she needs warmth and support now. I can provide that.

And so I nestle her close to me, tucking her under my chin and pulling the blankets and pillows up around us to shield her from the world.

Right now it's just her and I, and I need her to know that.

Chapter 22

Elodie

My eyes flick open, blinking against the bright light that floods in the room from the window. It's a sunny day today, a harsh contrast to the rain that usually graces the planet.

I'm warm, wrapped all up in a strong pair of arms. I don't want the feeling to end.

I squeeze my eyes back shut, but it's too late, Barre sees that I'm awake and attacks me with neck kisses.

"How are you feeling?" He murmurs against my ear carefully, as if a single syllable could break me in half.

I hadn't even thought of Locanas until this moment. I cringe, twisting away from Barre as memories grip me. I usually welcome my sweet rescuer's touch, but the overwhelming remembrance of my attacker causes sudden dizziness. I try to stumble out of bed, wrapped in a long blanket that causes me to stumble.

Barre is quick to pull himself from bed, in all his tall, shirtless glory. His eyes are flooded with concern as he reaches for me, I put my hand up for him to stop. He does, but not too far away from me.

"Tiny, you look unstable, let me hold you." His rough words sober me.

"Unstable?" I gawk at him, he quickly shakes his head.

"You look as if you'll fall over. I only wish to aid you. Always."

I smile softly at him, reaching out and gripping his forearms, because truth be told I'm not completely stable right now. He has reason to worry about my balance.

"I'm sorry, Barre. I just can't stop myself from being overwhelmed sometimes. I remember his hands on me, the heat of his skin and I..."

"And you.. Think that I am him?" My eyes snap up at the Rytarian that I trust with my life. The sheer pain etched into his face is enough to make my heart wrench.

I stand on my tip-toes to take hold of his shoulders.

"No, no. Of course not. But when it's so fresh, sometimes it's hard to tell anything apart. I just need some time. I'll get better, especially when we get out of here." I insist, and my assurance seems to calm him.

His large hands tentatively hold my wrists where they connect with his broad chest. I notice his effort to distance himself with any association with the monster that traumatized me.

"Speaking of going. We cannot, not until we figure out what is to be done with Locan.." I flinch. Barre clears his throat. "With the despicable excuse for a Rytarian."

I look down, suddenly nervous to face this whole situation.

"What is to be done with him?" I ask softly.

Barre shrugs under my touch. He's silent for a beat.

"There's been no decision. We should speak with the Emperor as soon as we can." He huffs in disgruntled annoyance. "The truth is that I wish to encourage execution, and I want to be the one to end him."

I gulp, hating the image of violence. I've never been one to stomach blood.

I can't imagine Barre being so volatile. He's just so gentle and kind, I would hate to associate him with any sort of pain and brutality. I have no doubt he's capable enough of it. He's covered head to toe in muscle, and he's taller than any other Rytarian I've encountered before.

"Okay. Then let's go talk to him. I want to go home."

Barre's dark eyebrows raise in surprise.

"I mean, I meant to say your home, of course, I didn't mean to suggest that I.."

He cuts me off by cupping my cheek and smiling down at me.

"It's as much my den as it is yours. Nothing would make me more happy than for it to be a home for you." His voice is brimming with joy, and my heart booms with warmth.

"I never thought I could be this happy. I never thought someone could love me the way you do." I admit, shame heating my cheeks as every cruel word spoken to me about my appearance comes back to me.

Barre stiffens, his face scrunching in confusion.

I try to hide my face automatically. My freckles are likely all too visible in the fresh light of morning shining through the windows.

Barre grabs my hands, pulling them away from my cheeks.

"What do you mean?" He demands, and I flinch, not knowing what to say.

A firm finger presses against the point of my chin, demanding my face to turn up and my eyes to meet his.

"Tiny, my sweet human, please tell me why you would think such a thing." His voice is even, concerned, any coarseness vanishing to make way for tenderness.

"Well, where I come from, my hair and my freckles... well... I am considered very ugly." I pause, and Barre's mouth drops open in shock. Before he can speak, I continue. "So much so that I was destined to live a life alone. No hope for a marriage, I mean, no hope for a mate. No one wanted their children to inherit my coloring. Since I was young I was taught to accept my fate. But then you came along."

I'm absolutely mortified by the end of my small speech. I want to run and hide. My secret is out, what if he decides to reject me too? Knowing now that I am a reject of society, he likely wants nothing to do with me, just like everyone else.

"They're fools. Every one of them." His words reverberate through me. I can't hide my shocked reaction. I gasp. He can't possibly think so. Can he?

"Wha.. what?" I ask quietly, taken aback.

For a second I think he's joking with me, but one look at his face and I see how serious he is.

"It would be a blessing for any of our kits to take after you. In looks and temperament. You are the most beautiful of any creature I've laid eyes on, and you're too kind for your own good."

A sweet kind of pain pangs in my chest. Butterflies erupt, batting their wings against my rib cage, making breathing difficult.

"But, surely you're put off by the fact that I'll always be seen as an outcast by my race, even the humans here on Rytaria. That type of prejudice would transfer to any of our children that get my red hair and freckles. Are you sure you could handle that kind of rejection?"

I practically choke trying to get each word out. I feel like I'm digging my own grave. A sob leaves my throat when Barre pulls me to his chest, lifting me off the ground as he crushes me to him.

"No, of course not, Tiny. I've never cared what society has to say of me, and trust me, they have said many things." I sniffle as he plays with the hair at my scalp, his fingers etched into the strands.

"Like what?" I press, desperate for any distraction from my sudden tears.

He's quiet for a while, before sighing and giving in.

"I am a gladiator."

I pull away to look at him, sniffling still.

"A what?"

"A gladiator. Or, I was. I would fight and kill in an arena for the entertainment of the public. Of course, I only fought criminals who committed capital offenses, sentenced to a fight to the death." He presses his lips together as I process what he's admitting to me. "I have never lost a battle. I ended each opponent."

I gulp, feeling uneasy. I can't picture my kind, sweet Barre hurting anyone. Then I remember Locanas after I was recovered from his clutches. I was too hysterical to notice the fight taking place, but I definitely saw the aftermath.

In all my life, I've never seen such brutality. And to think, it was all caused by Barre. Unfathomable.

"You.. you never lost?" I sound out the words, more so trying to get a grasp on the concept than actually asking him.

"My love."

"Yes?"

"Do you know what a threat level is?" I giggle, suddenly remembering.

"Yeah. Soleil said something about it when we were having our check ups. She had a translation chip, and our doctor was freaking out about our threat level. I have no clue what it means."

Barre shifts uncomfortably, slowly dragging me down his body as he places me on the ground.

"It's a basic ranking that a living thing has, rating how large of a threat it poses." He scratches the back of his head. "And humans, well, humans as far as we know have a threat level of 1. Which I didn't know until recently. I would've been more careful with you had I known. I thought you would be at least a 10."

I hold it in for a moment before choking on a giggle, and covering my mouth in embarrassment from the sound.

"A 1? That's hilarious. You must think I'm ultra fragile now." I laugh at myself, and the ridiculousness of the situation.

Barre doesn't look as amused as me. He cups my face in both of his warm, rough hands that swallow my cheeks. I cease my giggling and look up at him.

"Yes. You have no idea. I've never met someone with a threat level so low. And mine, well mine is the highest ever recorded. That is why it worries me." He breathes, and I feel my eyes widen.

"You mean.. You're the strongest thing on this planet?" I demand, and Barre swallows, hunching his shoulders as if he's ashamed. He nods.

"You don't understand, little female. I am like a god to these people."

A chill runs up my spine. I want to ask what his oh so impressive threat level is, but I'm honestly too afraid to pose the question.

"What that means is that mating me is like mating my reputation, my love. Eyes will follow us wherever we go. Everyone will know what I am capable of. Some will fear me, others try to challenge me, but most respect me."

I stare forward blankly. Everything he says feels too sudden, and I'm nearly overwhelmed with the information overload.

"Elodie." He murmurs. I look back up at him against my will as he uses his grip on my face to turn me towards him. "I would never, ever, hurt you. I would rather hurt myself. The only thing I will use my strength for from here on out is your protection. I only want to keep you safe. It would be my honor to keep you safe. It's as if my strength has purpose now. I can do good by being what you need."

Every word is like a kiss, every lilt of his deep voice like a warm blanket around my heart.

I guess I'm quiet for a while, because pretty soon Barre is shaking me a little.

"Elodie. Elodie, say something, tiny." He demands gruffly, and I grab him by the shirt, trying to drag him down to me. "What are you doing?"

"Come down here. Now."

He scoffs.

"Why?"

"So I can kiss you, bossy pants."

And just like that, he's on me, his lips meshed with mine as I show him just how much he means to me.

"Elodie, please sit." I tuck a stray piece of auburn hair behind my ear, looking at Barre uneasily as I slide into a chair. He smiles a small, reassuring smile before putting his hands on my shoulders as he stands behind me.

The pregnant, human Empress stands tall and regal ahead of me. She brought us into a small office room for this discussion.

Soleil and Fray are here, along with another human girl and her Rytarian mate. The girl holds a chunky baby in her arms, bouncing him on her knee as she glances around nervously. Her mate stands at her side, arms crossed over his broad chest. He looks pissed to just be here.

"I brought a friend to help discuss this.. Situation. Elodie, this is my friend Penelope." She gestures to the mousy girl who meets my eyes for a split second, smiles, and looks back down at her baby who gurgles as he shoves a chubby hand in his mouth.

"Hi." I say, waving slightly. She doesn't seem too talkative.

"Penelope and I were held captive on Earth by men who did.... Unspeakable things to us." She clears her throat, her robes sliding across her skin as she straightens, still so graceful in the face of an uncomfortable conversation.

I look down for a second, knowing that human men are capable of many horrible things.

"You see, I wanted Penelope and you here to discuss what's to be done about males such as those, males like

Locanas." I look away at the mention of that name, and Barre squeezes my shoulders a little too tightly.

"Assholes like that deserve to rot." Soleil exclaims, jumping out of her chair in anger.

The only reaction in the room is all the males nodding their heads in silent agreement.

"Let me dispose of him, your majesty, I beg of you." Barre raises his voice slightly, but the Empress raises a hand to get him to be quiet. I feel the tension blooming in him.

I put my hand on top of his, staring at the beautiful leader with baited breath. She smiles grimly at me.

"I have come up with an idea to ensure justice for any female wronged by a male in such a way. A male convicted of any sexual assault or any aggressive attack on a woman, the female in question may decide what is to be done with him." I'm speechless for a long time, sitting and marinating in the possibility. Something like that on earth would never be allowed.

"Of course, we still believe in innocence until proven guilty. But, when a male is tried and proven to have committed the assault, then his victim will choose his punishment. It only seems fair. And since there is no question of Locanas's guilt, you would choose what we do with him, Elodie."

I'm still silent, completely stricken and frozen in place. The only thing that finally thaws me is Barre kneeling in front of me. He grabs for my hands, holding them in his to garner my attention.

My eyes meet his own mismatched set, sizzling with determination.

"My love, please, allow me to end him. It would be a great honor to avenge you in such a way." He pleads with me, squeezing my fingers as the idea of inflicting harm makes his jaw tighten.

Everyone around us is silent, backing away from Barre as they are reminded just how dangerous he is. I gulp, feeling a bit nervous myself when I remember the conversation we had this morning.

Clearing my throat, I look up to the Empress.

"Can I.. can I think about it for a while? I'm not ready to make a decision quite yet." I ask, my voice sounding more like a croak than any language.

She smiles again, nodding gracefully.

"Of course. Take all the time you need."

Chapter 23

Barre

My neck is tense from how hard my jaw is locked in place. I stare down at the purpose for my life as she sits with the other human women. The Empress puts a gentle hand on Elodie's shoulder, smiling sweetly while she talks.

"I've told Penelope all about you. She was happy to come." The smaller human nods, looking shy but opening her mouth to speak anyway.

"Yeah. I knew I couldn't stand by and let another girl go through anything we did." The female named Penelope's voice is so small that I can barely hear her. The female looks like she's about to fall apart.

Her mate stands beside me, he holds their offspring in his arms, bouncing the kit lightly as he glares at the scene before us. Fray is on my other side, also watching his mate wordlessly.

"I didn't want to come, but now that we are here, there is clearly an issue." The kit holding male says to me, not looking away from his female.

I nod once, my fists clenching as I fight the urge to demand that Elodie let me kill Locanas.

"As much as I agree that letting a female decide what is to be done with a male who has attacked them, my Elodie is not in any shape to be making such a decision." I murmur, my prospective mate oblivious to our conversation. "I want to kill him."

The little kit babbles nonsensical words as he grabs at his Pa's hand.

"I understand. If it was my mate, I would have a difficult time restraining myself. How are you not killing him now?"

"I don't really know, myself. Ending him is all I can think about."

The male named Elik simply nods.

"You are a male worthy of her then. I know what everyone says about you, but as far as I'm concerned rumors are useless and damaging." Elik says, and his words resonate with me.

Many believe that I am a blood thirsty beast. A heathen god. I respect this male for not believing what others love to spread.

I stand up straighter, a new confidence settling in me.

"You are lucky to have a kit. It must be wonderful to be a Pa." I say, and he nods, a smile finally gracing his face as he looks down at his son.

"I am. It is the best feeling. He needs me, as does his Mama. Being needed, relied on, it is the only thing I want. You have a great future to look forward to."

One look at Elodie, and it's easy to believe him. She is my future. I can take on anything if she is at my side.

She catches me staring, and meets my eyes before smiling. She does a little wave my way before going back to the conversation around her.

"I think there might be some redemption for Locanas, if you so choose." The Empress admits, and even if she is a female I want to yell at her.

Everyone is allowed to make mistakes, but the ones Locanas made are not easily erased. No one can expect such mercy if they attempt what he did.

"No. I can guarantee no girls will feel safe if they hear what he did and know that he lives freely in the palace. Aren't we trying to make this place safe?" Little Penelope says, her voice gaining in confidence and volume.

The Empress nods, and Elodie chews on the inside of her cheek.

"She's right. That stupid bastard can't just do that and expect a mate to fall in his lap! If anyone knew he was a rapist, they would ditch his ass." Soleil interjects, arms folded over her chest as she grouches.

I have to agree with Elodie's friend. She makes sense.

"Yes, but if we are not a government of mercy, what does that say? We have to look at this from all angles." The Empress says. I roll my eyes silently.

Even if I disagree with her, she already makes a good leader. She is not blood thirsty and hungry to show her power.

"I'm not saying we just let Locanas go, but killing him? That seems a little rash. He needs to be punished harshly, of course, but death? I don't know."

To my shock, Elodie and Penelope nod. These humans are too squeamish. I have no problem with sentencing death. It is what I'm most accustomed to.

"Let's take a break, and get something to eat. I love ordering food, being pregnant allows me to be as lazy as I want." The Empress says suddenly, winking at Elodie before beckoning a guard over.

"If it were up to me, El, Locanas would be 6 feet under." Soleil remarks. I have no idea what that means.

My female laughs, but doesn't look pleased in the least.

"Thanks."

She stands, quickly making her way to me. She silently folds her arms around me, laying her orange head on my chest. I'm speechless.

I embrace her, not ready for the words she shares with me.

"I don't want you to kill him." She murmurs, and just as my body had relaxed, it tenses again. I lean back slightly, staring down at her.

Her face is set firmly, like she's completely sure of her decision. I'm still not convinced.

"You don't have to make a decision yet. You have more time to think it over, Tiny." I rub her arm to comfort her, as I glance from Fray to Elik. Both have troubled expressions. I take a deep breath. I suppose frustration is a part of having a female in your life. I will have to get used to this life if I am to take care of Elodie.

"But, don't you think he deserves some mercy? I don't know him well, but he's a person. I don't know. This is so stressful." Her eyes blur with tears, she tries to hide them in shame.

My jaw tightens as the muscle works, I despise seeing what this decision is doing to her. She is a young female, she does not have the capacity and training of laws and justice. She is massively intelligent and capable, as I've learned from being around her, but she should not be expected to decide something like this. Especially after what she has been through these past few days.

"My love, don't stress yourself right now. It hurts to see you faced with such a decision. Take your time."

"If I may.." I turn towards the voice, seeing the Empress and the other female, Penelope. They look at Elodie, small smiles on each of their faces.

"It may help if you were to... talk with Locanas. You can understand him now with your translator. Meeting him in his prison, safely behind bars, might help you make a decision. I'm sure you're very anxious to go home with your new mate."

The mention of the word mate does nothing to touch the anger I feel at the proposal. Elodie? Talking to Locanas? Unthinkable. The bastard does not deserve her company, and she doesn't need to look at him.

I open my mouth to tell them it's impossible, but Elodie speaks first.

"I like that idea. When?" I'm speechless at her agreement. I hold her a little tighter.

"Tomorrow would work best. You need to rest. I think this meeting has stressed you enough." The Empress takes Elodies hands in hers. "I know you will make a good decision, whatever it may be. We will be there with you every step of the way."

My little human smiles, but it doesn't quite reach her tired eyes.

Penelope suddenly moves to her mate, taking her kit from his arms and nestling his cheek with her nose. The offspring squeals with joy. Elik pulls his mate into his arms, smiling down at his family.

A path resounds deep in my chest as I glance back at Elodie. It seems as if our future is bright, but the fear of losing it is strong. I need to protect her from everything.

"I am taking my mate to our room. We will discuss this later."

Chapter 24

Elodie

After the doors close, I slip down on the couch, shoving my face into a pillow as Barre stalks around the room. Salsh nudges my elbow with his cold, wet nose. I groan, tucking myself in further to the cushions, wishing they would just swallow me whole.

I can tell that Barre is pissed. I don't want to deal with it.

"Elodie." He snarls. "I don't like this."

I huff into the pillow, biting the fabric as I clench my teeth. I know this. I know he hates Locanas and this whole situation. No one hates this more than me though. None of it's fair.

But when Empress Jane offered for me to talk with my attacker, it just felt right.

"I don't want you being near him."

I throw myself up into a sitting position, looking at the gladiator over the cushions.

He has his muscular arms crossed over his wide chest. His brooding expression would make a human man pee his pants, but to me he's simply an overgrown toddler throwing a tantrum.

"You think I want to see him? Don't be ridiculous. I have to make this decision. It wouldn't be fair to decide his fate without at least having a conversation with him." I demand, pushing the mass of red waves out of my hair in frustration.

Barre suddenly runs a hand over his stubble that has slowly turned into a beard.

"I don't want him to..."

I stand from the couch, tripping over my gown in my haste. I glare up at him, suddenly angry at his harsh tone. He's almost 2 feet taller than me, but I'm not intimidated.

Planting my hands on my hips, I stand up to him.

"What? You don't want him to what?" I demand, Barre glares, his jaw clenched tight.

"I don't want him to hurt you anymore. He scared you enough with his touch, his words will just make things worse." He scoffs, shaking his head. "And I don't want him to convince you to let him go free. He deserves death for what he's done."

I see the turmoil on his face, and hear the fury in his voice. I'm still getting used to understanding his words. We had so much wordless communication, I can read him like a book.

"He won't know that I get to decide his fate. At least, I don't think so."

I sigh, walking past Barre and towards the bed. I sink down, sitting on the edge and looking down at my hands.

"I like this idea that Jane has, I think it's fair, I'm just not in a great place to be making this decision."

A confused expression crosses his face.

"Jane?"

"The Empress." I provide.

I throw myself back on the bed, running my hands across the soft fabric beneath me and staring at the too ornate ceiling. I just want to be back in our little cabin in the woods.

"And yeah, Locanas" I choke trying to say his name, "did hurt me. Mentally, physically, but I need to know who he is. I haven't understood a thing out of his mouth. I need to know why he did what he did. I can't send a man to death without even knowing him."

Barre comes to stand in front of me. He chews on the inside of his cheek, turning to sit down next to me.

"You didn't understand me until yesterday." I hear the timidness trickle into his normally gravelly tone as the mattress dips beside me.

My head whips up, ready to tell him off. He dares to look dejected.

I grab his face, holding it tight and forcing him to look at me.

"That's different, I know you and you know that." I stare deeply into his eyes of two different colors, feeling like I've known him forever. Warmth spreads through me when a small reassured smile appears on his face.

But he doesn't look very convinced. There's worry in his face hidden in small places.

I bite my bottom lip, wanting to put my lips on his again.

"Speak your mind. I know you have a lot to say, I can see it." I press, grabbing for his hand and squeezing it.

Barre sighs, looking at the ground before returning his eyes to me.

"I also don't want him to think he has a chance with you. I don't want him looking and lusting over you. I see the way he looks at you. It brings out another sort of darkness I've never experienced. He needs to know you're mine, Elodie."

He delicately caresses my jaw and neck.

I feel my face pale at his words, realizing that this foreign feeling he's experiencing is jealousy and possessiveness. That sort of emotion is typically a red flag in human men, but knowing Barre the way I do, it comes from a good place.

According to Soleil, it's common in Rytarian males. I shouldn't be surprised.

A surge of butterflies erupts in my stomach. He loves me, Barre really loves me.

He suddenly lets go of my hand and neck, putting his head in his hands.

"I know, I am despicable for having these thoughts. Of course I'm more worried about you, after what he did, but there will always be a selfish side of me. I apologize."

Sorrow melts my heart at his stern tone. He's really beating himself up over this.

"Don't be so hard on yourself. Sure, you sound like a kid who doesn't want anyone looking at his favorite toy, but I understand." I rub his broad back, feeling the thick muscles ripple under my fingertips and trying not to drool.

He turns his head, peaking at me.

"Really?" He asks.

I nod exuberantly, smiling at him reassuringly.

"Yeah, if any girl, sorry, female started eyeing you like a snack I'd want to rip their eyes out. I'm somewhat of a gladiator myself."

He laughs, a deep raspy laugh that has me curling my toes.

"As much as I enjoy your violent sentiment, I cannot imagine you hurting anyone or anything." He muses, tucking a stray piece of hair behind my ear and then cupping my face, smiling down at me.

Yeah, I'm in trouble. I'm putty in this man's very strong hands.

"Hey, I might be a threat level 1, but I'm creative. I could take you on any day." I tease, and a gleam of mischief appears on his face. Oh no. What did I get myself into?

"Is that so?" He asks, tilting his head as he leans in closer.

"Yup. All it takes is a surprise attack."

"A what?"

I pounce on him, trying to push him down with no success. My arms go around his shoulders, pushing and tugging as I try to get purchase. Barre chuckles, falling back on the bed, pretending my attack has an effect on him.

I go for his hands, trying to get the upper hand, but suddenly I'm being jostled upside down until I'm completely under him. He's surprisingly gentle for his strength, but also quite firm as he grabs my wrists. He holds them in one massive hand, pinning them above my head.

Barre's grip is like steel, completely unbreakable. His hips press into thighs, holding me in place while he leans over me.

Not surprisingly, arousal blossoms as he presses a kiss to the side of my neck, holding my head in place with his other hand. The warmth of his body is melding with mine, overwhelming all my senses. I moan softly, unable to stop the noise from leaving my mouth.

Barre's face comes back up, a surprised look on his face, which quickly turns into a wicked, satisfied male grin. He bends down for more, nipping at my skin.

"Barre, I think I know the solution to this issue you have with Locanas."

He grunts in response, continuing his heavenly assault on the column of my throat. The tip of his nose bushes right under my ear, making the hair on the back of my neck stand on end.

"Maybe you should make me yours..fully." I taunt.

He freezes, slowly lifting his head out of the crook of my neck.

"Fully?" He barely manages to ask through clenched teeth.

"Does that make you mad?" I wonder, feeling like an idiot. Did I go too far this time? "If he sees your mark he'll know for sure I'm your mate, right? I mean, if you don't want to, I completely understa.."

I'm cut off when he pushes his lips to mine. The tip of his tongue delves into my mouth, brushing my bottom teeth. I'm a little too shocked to react. It doesn't take long before I'm moving in sync with him.

He pushes into me, holding himself up on his elbows and squeezing my wrists in his hand. I arch into him as I sigh into his mouth, sliding my tongue against his in a twist of lust.

The words going through my head the whole time becomes a mantra.

I love you. I love you. I love you.

I never thought I'd feel like this. I never thought I'd be able to share something like this with someone. I won't take it for granted.

Pretty soon, Barre is removing my clothes, and I tug at his. He fawns over my body, each new inch of skin revealed gets a reaction from him. He stops and kisses my flesh, looking at it with his hungry, mismatched eyes. The guy worships me with his eyes and gentle touch.

I love every moment of it, from the second he bits down on my neck, to the next when he takes me completely. I was already his, but this is real. This is permanent. It's everything at once and it's everything to me.

Chapter 25

Barre

The way down to the cells is long and cold, I walk closely behind Elodie, holding her hand and offering my silent support.

She is my mate now. Officially. My teeth made their mark on her neck, my scent wafts from her skin, my kit might already be planted in her womb.

The sheer male satisfaction coursing through me is enough to raise my confidence and puff my chest out as I walk. Even as we are on our way to see Locanas, I am confident, although I still want to tear his head from his shoulders.

I no longer worry about him looking at her like she's his. Last night I took her, and she gave herself to me. Elodie is mine and mine alone.

As the Emperor's guard unlocks the door to the underground prison, Elodie shivers in front of me. It could be the cold. It is rather chilly down here, and we're surrounded by thick concrete bricks to keep all warmth and comfort out. But, I know her shivers are from something more sinister.

I grab her shoulders, pulling her back to press against my front. She turns slightly to look up at me.

"It will be alright, tiny. I am here. He can't hurt you." Not if he wants to live, I silently add, but don't dare speak it out loud.

She simply nods, turning away from me as the heavy door swings open.

"You don't have to do this. No one is forcing you." I murmur before I let her continue forward. Elodie sighs, nodding.

"I know." She responds, stepping into the darkness without another word.

I follow behind her quickly, glancing around the dim prison hallways. When I spot Locanas in his cell, I growl, and Elodie swiftly grabs for my hand. As she squeezes my fingers, I wonder if she's doing it to calm me or to bring her comfort, maybe a bit of both.

The criminal stands from his small nest, clamoring over to the bars of his cell. His desperate eyes are locked onto Elodie.

The Emperor and Empress are close by, quietly observing unless they need to intervene. The Emperor has his arm wound tightly and protectively around his mate's waste, his li ng, ring covered fingers anxiously brushing the pregnant bump that holds his kit.

"You're here. I.." Locanas begins, but as his hands wrap around the bars, his nostrils flare. His pupils dilate. Our species has a good sense of smell. He's putting it together in his mind. Good. Let him figure it out.

Suddenly he stops, attempting to shake the prison bars holding him captive. They remain where they are, but Elodie jumps back in alarm.

"You took her! You bred her!" He yells, absolutely fuming with anger. "You had no right."

His accusations have no effect on me. What he says is true. My only worry is how his words may affect my mate. I put a hand on her shoulder to comfort her with my presence.

"That may be so, but I had more right than you." I chuckle darkly, pulling Elodie to lean back against my chest. "Unlike you, she asked me to please her. I had her consent to make her my mate."

Locanas glares at me, and I'll gladly take his anger. As long as his attention is on me, my little human will feel safer. This is always my intention.

"This isn't about him." Her sweet, lulling voice drifts through the cold room, filling it with sunlight and warmth. I wasn't expecting the amount of confidence ringing in her tone, but it's there and it's powerful. It's a display of her inner strength, a show of the way she won't let what he did destroy her.

That's my female.

Pride swells in my chest for her.

"This is about you, Locanas. I've never been able to speak to you. Now, I have a translation device, and you no longer have power over me. I'm not scared of you anymore." She insists, but I hear her voice waver the slightest bit at the end. I pray to the gods that Locanas didn't pick up on it. She needs this.

Locanas's eyebrows scrunch in distaste.

"I never wanted you to be scared of me. Never."

Elodie steps forward, too close to him for my comfort. I let her go anyway.

"Then why? Why torture me? Why follow me and touch me and terrify the crap out of me! Why?" She demands, fury in her little voice, bravery stiff in her stance.

"I didn't know. I am sorry. I... I realize now my mistake, and I know I do not deserve mercy. I can't be around females. I realize now that I don't know enough about females to have a mate. I don't want to hurt anyone else with my ignorance. Send me away."

I clench my jaw, wishing to end his life here and now. That would certainly keep him away from females permanently. I step forward to stand next to my mate, looking down at her face.

She has her infuriatingly tempting bottom lip wedged between her teeth in concentration.

Thankfully, the Emperor clears his throat and steps forward. He reaches out a hand to touch Elodies shoulder, but spots the fresh mark on her neck and pulls his hand back. He likely knows from experience how possessive I feel after making her mine. He glances at me meekly, and apology in his gaze.

The same can't be said for Locanas.

"I just wanted you, Elodie. How can you not realize this?" He says, gripping the bars that keep him captive until his knuckles turn white.

She fiddles with her dress nervously, and for a moment I think she doesn't know what to say.

"I knew, Locanas, trust me, I knew. The way you went about it was all wrong, you scard me. Your strength, your disregard for my fear, it was too much. In my eyes you were a monster." Her timid voice is even and confident despite the lack of volume.

Locanas's face falls. His jaw goes slack, and everyone awkwardly stands aside. No one wants to interfere, but it is n ot an easy thing to watch.

"You were afraid of me?" He asks, as if this is the first time he considered such a thing.

A strong part of me wants to burst out in anger at the idiocy of such a statement. Of course she was afraid of him! Is he unable to read emotions like a normal individual? How can he so easily ignore a females's terror at his mere presense.

"How did you not notice?" Elodie demands. The male twice her height shrinks, his spine curling as he hunches himself over to seem less intimidating. I've seen it all so many times 9n the battle ring. My opponents often tried to seem weak to throw me off. It never worked.

"A male, a male in the cafe told me that the way you acted, the noises you made and your facial expression were a sign of arousal. I was a fool to believe him, but it gave me hope, and so I convinced myself that he was telling the truth. I hoped that one as beautiful as you would want me for a mate." Embarrassment floods his face. "I was wrong. I am sorry."

Elodie stiffens, and the Emperor strides forward towards the holding cell.

"This male, what was his name?"

"I do not remember, I only met him in passing." Locanas looks down. "If you choose to execute me, I understand. I do not want to go on living."

I am unable to tell if he is being earnest. I will gladly give him death if that's what he desires. I wont make it quick, either. I would draw it out, make sure he feels every ounce of pain I purposefully inflict on his pathetic body. I would shatter every piece of him that dared press against my mate. Break every bone and muscle that held her in place against her will. I would make him feel all the terror he inflicted on her, and more.

My desire to maim is cut short by the soft touch on my arm.

"I'd like to go now." The sweet, tender words whispered up at me make me pause, glancing down at my mate as the heated anger floats away, replaced by a tender longing I only ever associate with my sweet Elodie.

"Of course." I put my arm over her shoulders. She leans into me as I lead her away from her attacker. He drops to his knees as we all leave him in the darkness.

No one speaks to Elodie. Jane eyes her carefully, as if she will break. She will not shatter though, my sweet human, she is all silent strength. I do not care if her threat level is 1. She will always be strong to me.

"We will gather later to discuss, yes?" The Emperor pleads, looking nervous. My jaw clenches. I want to speak with him privately. I eye him purposefully, hoping to convey my wishes while I rub Elodies arm in comfort.

"Dearest, why don't you take Elodie to her and Barre's den. I must have a word with him."

Elodie shoots me a tired smile as Jane links their arms together and leads my mate down the hallways.

The Emperor and I stand side by side silently, watching our mates walk away until they disappear around a corner. Now that they are completely out of ear range, I speak.

"He must die."

The Emporor sighs.

"I know." He rubs his face, stress obvious on his sharp features. "You must know that this new law will not work. As much as I want my mate to have a say in our ways, humans are so different. They are far too forgiving. I've kept my mouth shut too long. Locanas has made an unforgivable mistake. I do not want him around any females."

"I want him dead, your majesty." I insist, and he nods.

"Yes. It will be done. One way or another, he cannot be allowed to go on."

I nod, satisfaction swelling at his admission. As much as I want to beg that I be the one to end my mate's attacker, I keep my mouth shut.

Everything in time.

Chapter 26

Elodie

I'm fast asleep when a thundering knock sounds at the door. I stretch, my limbs sliding against the smooth sheets. My naked skin prickles with warmth as a hand slides slowly up my back. It's a big hand. I grin at the reminder.

Barre is sitting up above me, eyes alert as he stares at the door where the sound just emanates from. He's naked too. Of course he is. We made love twice last night. I grin into my pillow, hugging it to my chest as I roll onto my back.

"Who is it?" I wonder aloud. Barre grunts, running his hand continuously up and down my arm, plunging his fingers into my hair and massaging my neck.

"I don't know, but I don't care to find out." He responds, his gruff face covered in the early morning light.

I lift my hand to touch his lips that are still pink and swollen from my kisses.

I grin. Maybe that can be my form of a mark. My teeth are far too dull to pierce his skin.

Another knock echoes through the room, and my master groans gruffly as he stands swiftly from bed. I turn just in time to see his tanned, toned backside as he stomps to the door completely naked.

A blush floods my cheeks, and I cover my cheeks with my hands. His butt is absolutely perfect.

"Good gravy." I mutter under my breath, plopping back into bed, covered in red waves of hair that fan out all around me, a stark flash of color against the white sheets.

I don't pay much attention to the conversation at the door, I simply burrow into the covers like a hibernating animal. I'm content and sleepy, ready to doze back off any second. My body is sore but thrumming with glee. I just want whoever it is to go away and not come back. I want Barre all to myself. He makes me forget that there's even a world outside of here.

The door closes, and my mate returns quickly, gently touching my shoulder.

"My love, you need to get up and get dressed." I shoot him a look to show him my displeasure. He chuckles.

"I know, but it is important." He pets my hair, pushing it from my sleepy face. "I wouldn't pull you from the nest unless it was important."

I nod, wondering what on earth could be going on. I start to pull my clothes on, but Barre stops me for a quick but heated kiss, letting go of me to get dressed himself. I stand still for a moment. I'm still completely in awe of this between us.

It's a dream come true.

When we're finally dressed, and sure we can keep our hands off of each other, Barre opens the door and The Emperor struts in in all his gilded glory. I freeze, my limbs going rock hard as he makes himself at home by sitting on the couch. He looks far too shiny and important to be laid back so casually.

He motions for me to sit across from him, his expression grim.

So, he's here to discuss Locanas. I was afraid this would happen.

"Please sit, Elodie."

"I haven't decided what to do with him yet." I blurt out, clutching my arms to my body to try to appear as small as possible as anxiety finds a home in my chest.

Barre is quick to come up beside me and put his hands on my shoulders, turning me towards him. I don't look him in the eyes, too afraid of what I'll see in his mismatched eyes. I know he wants Locanas dead. I also know that he's frustrated with me for not making a decision yet. I'm stalling, and he knows it.

His warm hand goes under my chin, tipping it up until I'm forced to look way up into his handsome face.

He pretty much had a full beard when we woke up yesterday, but he shaved it off. I'm not used to seeing his bare jaw yet. It's so sharp it could cut diamonds. I don't expect the compassion I see, but I should have, he's too sweet.

"It's alright, Tiny. The Emperor is just here to offer a solution. Just listen to him, alright? There is no pressure for you to decide right away, alright?" Voice calm and even, Barre's words make me nod my head.

He always knows what to say to reassure me.

Taking a deep breath, I address the elephant in the room, or should I say the Emperor in the room. I sit across from him in a large chair. Before I can settle, Barre comes over and picks me up with one arm, taking my seat and nestling me in his lap.

Calm reassurance washes over me, and I'm now 95% ready to talk with the plante's leader.

"Elodie, as you know, Locanas admitted guilt and wants to be punished. As you also know, us Rytarians do not take such a crime lightly. If it were up to me or your mate, Locanas's head would be hanging over the castle gates, showing every male here what we do to rapists."

I shutter at his words, wanting to escape this conversation already.

Barre narrows his eyes.

"Easy. My mate does not like violence."

The emperor releases an exasperated sound.

"I am just saying what both of us were thinking." He defends himself, holding his hands up, each knuckle decorated with a ring. His nails are short but elegantly rounded, painted a deep blue color.

I look up at my mate, confirming that he agrees with the Emperor's thoughts. He bites the inside of his cheek, but he doesn't disagree. I turn my head down. The thought of someone's head being torn off freaks me out. The more I consider it, the more queasy I get.

"See what you did? She is too delicate for this."

"I am not! I'm fine!" I'm really not, but I hate being treated like a piece of glass.

They're both silent for a while before I clear my throat.

"Go on." I encourage, and the Emperor nods his head reluctantly.

"Well, I want to launch an investigation into who told Locanas this false information about females. Obviously, in the wrong hands, this information has led to you being attacked. I don't want a repeat of that. Locanas was too naive and uneducated to know better. While I want to gladly end his life, I can't exactly do this until we find out who told him these lies. I need him alive, but I don't want him in the city, or anywhere near the humans we've brought here. So, I have thought of a solution I would like you to consider."

His reasoning makes sense, and I can't explain the pain in my gut, even as Barre's arms tighten around me.

"We have a distant continent, far from our main land, it is covered in mountains, it's called Kalinda, and it is where we once mined for precious metals, the most important being malikondite. Once our society panicked over the loss of females, this metal was no longer mined as it once was, because it wasn't needed anymore. The main thing we used it for was translation devices. We didn't think we needed anymore because..."

"Because the population wouldn't continue." I finish his sentence for him.

The Emperor nods solemnly, staying quiet for a pause before continuing.

"Now that we have lots of females in need of translation devices, we need to continue harvesting the malikondite. The only thing is that it is very secluded. So, I have been thinking of a solution, and I think I have found it with our predicament."

Barre caresses my neck, pulling my t-shirt back to look at the mark on the soft spot between my throat and neck. He grins. It's so sexy, I'm almost too distracted to keep my mind on track.

What were we talking about again? Oh yeah, Locanas.

"So, what does this have to do with Locanas?" I wonder aloud, trying to calm my breath as Barre continues to subtly touch me and turn me on so bad that my head is swimming. Based on his smile and lazy eyes, I know that he knows exactly what he's doing to me.His big body is rock solid under me, nothing like my own trembling pile of limbs that want to crumble under his fingers.

"We can make the mountains of Kalinda a place to send criminals. They have no choice but to work mining the mountains. Locanas would be the first. He would be far away from any females, and he would live a solitary life." The Emperor shrugs, looking like he's restraining his excitement at his idea. "And, of course, we would get the malikondite we need. Send some males every now and then to collect the metal and check on Locanas, I can even call him if I have more questions about this gossiper in our midst."

The way he explains it makes everything fall into place, like this was the missing solution all along, a puzzle piece clicking perfectly. Not killing Locanas, but not ever having to see him again, and never having to worry about him.

I gulp, questions buzzing around my brain.

"What if he escapes?" My voice is tentative, small. I sit up straighter, clamoring to get away from my mate as he moves to touch my neck and further play with me like a toy. He knows all the buttons to press, and I can't deal with it right now. This is an important decision to make.

The Emperor is already shaking his head.

"The continents are separated by a large, fresh water ocean. He wouldn't have a boat, and he would not be able to swim across the ocean." He assures me. "Not to mention, he seems sincere in his regret. He asked to be punished. I doubt he would try to escape his imprisonment."

It's comforting, but I still feel uneasy, scared of the male that hurt me. As long as he's under the same roof as me, I will not be able to fully relax.

Turning into the solid warmth that Barre offers, I play with the collar of his shirt as I look trustingly up at him, feeling semi-safe in his arms.

"What do you think? Does it seem like a good idea?" I ask him.

He gives me a small smile.

"It's up to you."

"I still want your opinion. Just because you have a penis doesn't mean you shouldn't help decide."

Barre's eyes grow wide. The Emperor coughs. I chuckle.

"Well," My mate starts thoughtfully, clearing his throat. "I would prefer killing him, but this seems to be the next logical decision if you don't want me to kill him."

"I don't want you to kill him. I guess this is what we should do, right? It seems like the best course of action. I want him far away. That way, I won't have to be scared of him anymore, and he can't hurt anyone else."

Both enormous rytarian males nod at my words, and it helps to sound out my thoughts and have them understand. I crack my knuckles in my lap as I continue to weigh it in my mind.

"What are you..? What is that?" My eyebrows furrow in confusion as I look up at Barre. He seems disgusted.

"What?" I hold up my hands. "This?"

I crack more knuckles, the crunching sound making him cringe as he covers my fingers, trying to put an end to the habit with the strength of one of his hands. It reminds me of when he pinned my arms over my head last night while he..

"Don't do that. It's horrible. I cannot stand it." Barre insists, and I laugh, shaking my head in amusement.

"Dude wants to tear off someone's head, no problem, his mate cracks her knuckles and all of the sudden he's squeamish."

"My name is not dude."

That earns another laugh from me, and then he's tickling me, making me hunch over as the giggles take over. The Emperor tells us he'll make the arrangements for Locanas before he lets himself out, leaving us to ourselves.

I thought when he left I would want to go back to sleep, but as Barre carries me back to bed, better ideas start to form of what we can do to pass the time.

Chapter 27

Barre

I shoulder through the large, wooden doors that lead to the launch pad. Too many spaceships and aircrafts populate the rough ground. Some are obsolete hunks of garbage that haven't been used in centuries.

As i walk past the countless ships, my boots thumping, I reach out and run my hand across the large metal sides of a rusty ship dotted with holes.

Our race used to send out countless spaceships to explore other worlds, even more when our females died out, and now these ships sit around for the most part. Other than the few that fly out to do our regular trade of goods with other planets, there is no need to leave the safety of Rytaria, especially now that we must protect the precious females we have harbored here.

"Barre!" Fray is stalking towards me, arm outstretched to clap me on the shoulder in greeting, but Salsh growls fiercely, always at my side and ready to protect. I roll my eyes.

Fray stops short, hands held up in a sign of peace.

"He wants to protect you. He doesn't know how powerful you really are." That earns a chuckle from me. "I'm so glad that you could make it. I know it is early."

I nod, looking ahead as we walk side by side, heading to our destination together. Salsh is quick to follow, never straying far from my legs.

"It was not easy to pull myself from the nest." I respond, even though I had to be here, it is true. I could hardly get myself to leave Elodie's side for even a moment of time. She is my life now. I had to station 3 guards outside our door to ensure her safety until I return.

I have never been paranoid. My power often secures anything I want or need, I've never had to worry. I had nothing to lose either, but now that story has changed completely. I have everything to lose because I have Elodie. She is everything. I've never known such fear, such ecstasy and love, such paranoia. Its all a lot. It was easier before she came along, but I wouldn't change it for anything. I hope the complications never stop if this is what love is.

Fray laughs at me, breaking me from my haze.

"What did you say?" I ask, slightly embarrassed.

He shakes his head.

"I was just telling you that I understand completely. Getting a female changes you, it is hard to leave the sanctuary they offer." He grins, shaking his head and running a hand through his white hair. "But, it seems like you were already thinking about that."

Clearing my throat, I look away as I think of my time with my sweet, tiny mate. She is sunshine wrapped in red hair. Sanctuary is the perfect word to describe her. It would not be noble for me to comment further to Fray on why exactly I struggle leaving her. I cant say how I belong between her thighs, and no matter how many times we tussle in the nest, she is still never satiated.

I always leave her satisfied, but she is always hungry for more.

I try to contain my smile, ready to get back to my fiery goddess.

"Well, regardless, I am glad you are here. It is your right to send him off." Fray says, and I nod, knowing that it is also Fray's right to see Locanas shipped off to the mountains of Kalinda.

Locanas was Fray's second in command, I can only imagine how hard it is to trust a male and watch him become a dishonorable monster.

We continue walking silently until we come to a rather large air ship at the end of the strip. It's bustling with a few males as they prepare for flight. They carry supplies up the ramp and into the ship. They're all preparing to ship of this criminal so that none of us have to worry about him again.

Speaking of the criminal, I spot him at the bottom of the ship, hands chained together and eyes glued to his feet.

Locanas's jaw is clenched tight. He doesn't want to be here. I can't blame him for that, but he deserves this. Actually, he deserves far worse, but this is mercy as far as I'm concerned. At least he's not dead.

"Are you ready to board, Locanas?" Fray's voice, once friendly and light, is now filled with storm clouds as he directly addresses the male that is the reason why we are here. His tone leaves no room for discussion.

We are sending him. He has no choice in the matter.

He looks up. The male that frightened my female. The reason she ran terrified into the woods, hurting herself and crawling into a tree. If I hadn't of found her when I did, she would have died, I have no doubt about that.

Remembering the day I came across her in the woods, her sad eyes and wet hair, I know now that even then I realized that my life would change forever.

The real question is, how can I hate Locanas when he is the reason I found my life's purpose? Elodie would've never found me way out on my land if she didn't run for her life from this male.

I can't exactly thank him. The trauma he inflicted is still not okay.

"Yes." He takes a small step forward, glancing from Fray to me quickly. His expression shifts.

"Barre. I... I want to say that I'm sorry." He says slowly, and I can tell as he forces the words out that they are hard to admit for him, but they seem genuine.

I don't accept the apology.

"I'm not the one you need to make amends with. She will decide if she will forgive you. Not me."

He nods, looking down once more, his jaw tight and lips thin. Locanas has accepted his fate it would seem. That makes things a whole lot easier.

"You disappointed me, Locanas. I thought you could shape into a worthy male. A male of honor and integrity. Instead, you frightened a female and likely caused her lifelong fear in her mind. This is no minor crime. For that you are sentenced to hard labor. What say you?"

The males around us slow their work, greedy to overhear what the prisoner has to say in response to his sentence. I shoot them one glance to tell the to get back to work, and they quickly listen, hustling away with their chores.

Locanas squares his shoulders.

"I gladly accept. I can only hope that death will take me soon." He says, and I nod in agreement.

Fray cocks his head to one of the guards, and soon the prisoner is led up the ramp, his fate sealed in a few moments.

"I didn't need to be here for this." I say. "He'll probably die out there anyway."

"Yes, you did." Fray turns to me, disregarding Salsh as the rasler begins snarling. "I knew it would be comforting to see him leave. It'll give you peace of mind."

I don't know how Fray knew this, but he's right. It does oddly make me relax to watch the ship rumble to life, prepared to fly Locanas very far away where we will never have to deal with him ever again.

The ship's hatch finally closes up, sealing up the ship and everyone in it. Fray and I take several steps backwards, watching as the ship thrums. The ship lifts into the sky, sending dirt and pebbles scattering around our feet. I cover my eyes with a hand to my forehead, narrowing them as Locanas floats away.

Fray turns to me, hands on his hips. I don't look at him, keeping my eyes focused on the ship until it takes off, heading towards the horizon until it becomes a distant little dot in the sky.

"You don't have to stay if you don't want to." Fray begins, stalking back to the castle. I watch him and follow behind him. "Although, it would be safer for your female if you were to live here."

I growl under my breath and shake my head.

"No."

The idea of spending the rest of my life in the palace puts a pit in my stomach. Every minute here is another minute spent suffocating.

Fray shoots me a disapproving glance.

"She would be better protected here. The walls, the guards. It would be wiser to keep her here rather than dragging her back out to your cabin."

I stop dead, grabbing the male by the collar and pulling him until we're face to face.

"Are you saying I can't protect my own mate?" I spit, insulted buy the mere implication.

Frays eyes are wide, flicking down to Salsh who is foaming at the mouth before looking back at me.

"No, no I am just trying to tell you she would be safer here, where we can all keep an eye on her." He tries to defend himself but the damage is already done.

Uncertainty funnels into my head, and it doesn't show any signs of slowing down.

My pride kicks in, trying to fight back against the intrusion of self doubt.

"I have the highest threat level of any creature on this planet and the next." I crack my neck to one side, signalling I'm ready for battle at any moment if he wishes to threaten me.

Fray gulps.

"154. You remember don't you? Now, I'm not sure what your threat level is, Fray." I look him up and down, assessing his strength with my trained, gladiator eyes. "115? Maybe 120?"

He clears his throat.

"117."

"117." I repeat, amusement in my voice. I know I'm embarrassing him, but I can't seem to care. "Alright. So, maybe with my threat level I'll be able to manage protecting Elodie. Certainly better than someone with 117. Okay?"

Fray is silent for awhile, his jaw flexing as he thinks.

"I'm just trying to help. Elodie is very important to my mate."

"Elodie is everything to me. I will ensure she is safe and happy."

Fray nods, and that's all I need. I let him go and head inside. My breathing is still harsh and panicked. My hands are shaky, mind hazy.

Salsh whines, nudging my palm with his snout. I ignore him. I'm focused on getting back to my mate. I need to ensure she's safe to ease my mind, and I need her touch and ease my body. Most of all, I need her sweet voice to comfort my heart.

Chapter 28

L o -
canas

I stare vehemently at the ground, wishing more than anything that it would swallow me up whole. There's a guard on either side of me, they carry my elbows tightly in their grips, making sure I don't even attempt to escape.

They have to be careful. I don't blame them.

The hallways of the ship are cold. It's an atmosphere I'm used to. I served on many missions, stalked down many metal hallways of countless ships. Things have changed since then.

Back then, I was second in command on those ships. The males that walked past me would bow their heads, too afraid to make eye contact with their superior.

Now, I wear cuffs. My hands are bound tightly in front of me, the cuffs biting into my wrists.

The few males we pass as I'm brought down the halls stare at me, no fear in their eyes. No. They look at me with disgust. Hatred. Shame.

I deserve those all those stares, every single sneer. I am a monster. A villain. A bad guy.

"Alright, Locanas, here is where you will be staying." One of the guards says, shoving me through an open door that leads to the storage room. There are countless crates of varying sizes, stamped with labels.

Some have food rations, others are marked as mining tools.

Of course. Tools. I'm being sent away for hard labor, that's my sentence. This is my purpose now.

Across from the wooden crates is a small holding cell. The space is tiny, and looks as if it was just installed. I roll my eyes at the cramped place that's supposed to hold me until we reach my permanent prison in the mountains of Kalinda.

The barred door to my cage swings open, the shining, clean hinges hardly squeaking. I'm roughly shoved inside by both guards, I stumble but quickly regain my footing. I turn to them before they can shut me in, sticking my foot as the door shuts on my toes. I don't even wince.

Silently, I raise my hands in front of me, cocking my head to my wrists.

One of the guards backs away as the other sighs, digging into his pocket and fishing out a key. He quickly unlocks me. My grip goes free, and I roll my wrists to ease the tightness in the joints and bones.

I politely remove my foot, allowing myself to finally be locked inside the holding cell. I observe my little, temporary home. The small nest is pushed against the back wall with a thin, blue blanket and pillow strewn carelessly across the mattress. A toilet and sink sit in the corner.

That's all there is. It's simple, but comfortable.

I walk to my nest, sitting on it and resting my elbows on my knees. The situation is sinking in. Placing my face in my hands, I sigh. After days spent in my holding cell in the dungeons, I've had time to realize what I've done.

My crime is no minor thing. I deserved the death Barre wanted to award me. Instead, somehow, I'm being sent to another continent to serve hard labor. I'll be in complete isolation. A lonely life in the mountains.

I lay back on the cramped nest, staring at the ceiling. The metal paneling above me is gray and drab, reminding me of old times sitting in my own quarters. Then I was surrounded by small luxuries I took for granted. Now, I have nothing to my name.

As the ship roars, engines humming and bustling, I try to calm myself with deep, settling breaths. My stomach drops as we take off, hovering from the safety of the palace. The familiarity of the main land, Kilig, where I was born and grew up. I will never be back.

It's my own doing. I don't deserve to be sorrowful over this. Not being sentenced to death was a mercy I did not earn.

I suppose females are too kind. It was Elodie that chose this for me, as was her right. She was the human I wronged. The beautiful little creature with red hair is still fresh in my memory. Realizing her cute expressions were not a reaction of desire, but a result of her fear, tears me apart inside.

I have been a fool.

I will never see a female ever again.

A sudden clanking sound startles me, and I sit up quickly, glancing around the crates sharply. Something pushes against a water barrel. The sound of rustling finally urges me to stand up and walk to the bars, curious to see what is happening.

My eyes find a small grate from the air vent. The cover is laying on the ground. I grip the bars tightly.

A little head pops up, and my mouth falls open in disbelief.

The female raises an eyebrow at me.

"What are you staring at? You're the one in a jail cell." She says, her voice snarky. She crawls over to a crate and looks closely at the label with narrowed eyes. "How do you even read these? Your language is just little dots. So weird."

I'm still not over my shock enough to even attempt speaking.

She clambours to stand on her feet. I realize quickly she's only as tall as the smallest crate. Gods help me. She's tiny. Her hair is so short she looks like a young male, the strands standing up in brown waves and spikes.

"What does this say?" Her face scrunches at the label, pointing at it with a stubby finger.

"Rations." I grunt, eyeing her up and down as my grip on the bars grows tighter. "What are you doing here? On this ship?"

The stowaway pays me no mind as she attempts to pry open the case with her bare hands. She tweets with effort as the box stays still. It doesnt even budge.

"Crap. How am I supposed to live off of snacks?" She mumbles to herself, walking to another crate and pushing at it.

Nothing.

"Answer me, female." I command, but she won't even look at me.

"Female this, female that. Is that all you guys know how to say?" She huffs with laughter, shrugging a shoulder. "And don't even get me started on teats."

I feel my face heat. Did she just say teats? What's wrong with that word?

Shaking my head to dislodge the distractions, I clear my throat.

"I'll ask you again, what are you doing here?" I press, but she just laughs at me, continuing to attack the boxes without success. Being ignored like this is infuriating.

"Answer me. Why are you here?" I raise my voice, trying to get across the urgency of the question.

Without turning her face to me, she raises her hand, all of her fingers down except the middle one, it's sticking up at me. Even though she's partially turned away from me, I can see the smirk on her face.

What an odd gesture.

"I don't know what that means."

"Of course you don't, your skull is thicker than concrete." She muses, and I narrow my gaze on the tiny thing. She has to be the shortest human I've ever seen. Her short hair makes her look even smaller.

"Yes. My skull is thick, all of my bones are strong. I am a warrior." I announce.

She shakes her head, her brown waves bouncing.

"Were a warrior. Looks like you're a prisoner now." The human female makes a tisking sound with her pretty mouth, her lips thin but oh so pink.

"You are correct about one thing, I am a prisoner, but I am still a warrior."

She grins, finally abandoning her hopeless task of breaking open a crate. The female walks to me slowly. She's so small I have to strain my neck to look down at her.

"What are you in for?" She wonders, so close that I stutter on my words.

No. No more females. I am a monster. I shouldn't be speaking to her, let alone looking at her beautiful, round face.

"I cannot tell you, but just know it is very bad."

She sighs in disappointment, her shoulders slumping.

"Well, I can't exactly tell you why I'm here if you don't tell me. That's sort of a double standard." She tells me, beginning to walk back to the vent, and frustration builds.

I want to grab her, the urge so strong I think if this barrier were not in the way, I might act on it.

The thought startles me. No! I cannot keep entertaining these thoughts. I will not indulge the monster inside me.

"Wait!" I call, just as she is about to crawl back in her tunnel.

She turns to look at me over her shoulder, on her hands and knees, her deliciously rounded rump facing me.

"What?" She asks, exasperated.

"Will I see you again?" I ask, telling myself it's simply a result of my worry for her safety. Another voice, deep inside me, knows that it is a request that comes from the selfish monster. The monster that wants to eat this female up with it's hungry gaze. It's aching ears long to hear each word she has to share.

But no, it must only be because of her safety. That is all that matters. I should not be looking at females... and enjoying it. I should sooner pluck my eyes out.

The female shrugs in response, flashing me a smile.

"Bye." She says, turning and shimmying back into the vent, grabbing the grated cover and pulling it back into place.

I pick up a few sounds of her journey through the passage, but soon it disappears with all other traces of her.

Chapter 29

Elodie

I never thought I would ever be escorted off the premises of anywhere, let alone like it. Yet here I am, hand in hand with Barre. A guard holds our bags as he strolls us to the front door of the palace. He carries the big pack Barre brought with us originally, and the one I got while staying in the palace. It's much smaller.

Inside the bag is a whole new wardrobe tailored to me. I made sure to choose dresses that would be ideal for living in the woods. Low maintenance sun dresses, loose fitting wide leg pants, long sleeve t-shirts. I got to pick out everything. It was the highlight of my week.

I shoot a sly glance at Barre. Well, not the biggest highlight, that's for sure.

Before too long we're stepping into the sun, letting the warm rays beat down on us. There's no rain today. It's bright. Too bright. I thought I would bask in the joy of a sunny day. I had looked forward to a day like today.

Now though, now I'm missing the rain so much my chest aches. I love the smell of it, the sound of it.

"It'll be back, tiny, don't worry." I look up at my mate, curious. Barre laughs. "The rain. You're glaring at the sun. I know you miss the rain. I do too. It never leaves for long, so don't worry, okay?"

He clamps a hand on my shoulder, squeezing it in reassurance. He already knows me so well. I definitely made a good choice. I smile to myself, knowing this life will be good to me with Barre in it.

Salsh runs forward, and I know he's spotted something. That's when I see Soliel running to me, arms open, but our pet has the gall the step in front of her before she can get to me. He stands solidly in front of me, paws spread in a wide stance as he growls at my best friend.

"Hey, puppy I'm just trying for a goodbye hug." She insists, letting her arms drop pathetically.

I chuckle, because it's hilarious that he thinks that Soleil could hurt me. She's smaller than me, and drained of energy because she's pregnant. Although, even then, she could probably beat me in a fight easily.

"Salsh." Barre commands, and his companion reluctantly leaves me, going to sit beside my mate with an annoyed sigh.

Soliel crashes into me, and I hold her close, my arms wound tightly around her neck and burying my face in her dark hair.

"I'll always love you, no matter what. You have to come visit me, especially when the kit gets here." My usually stoic best friend sniffles in my ear, and I pull away, my hands still on her back as I assess her puffy eyes.

"Kit? You already adopting the lingo?"

Soleil laughs a little laugh, wiping at her nose with the inside of her wrist.

"I guess so. It's Fray's fault." Another tear rolls down her cheek, and I feel my own eyes start to sting in response.

"Don't cry! I can't handle it when you cry." I mumble, pushing away the moisture collecting in my eyes. It's stubborn and decides to keep flowing anyway.

"Yeah, I think the last time you saw me cry was when I got grounded for painting a pair of boobs on the side of the main building at home. Man, I got in so much trouble."

I start cackling, remembering the words "Pussy Power" written in pink paint over the cartoon boobs on the red brick wall. Our old home was strict, and Soleil liked to disobey, I was always too afraid to step out of line.

"I wish I had helped, I was too much of a goody two shoes." I admit, and Soliel nods as she laughs, still rubbing the tears from her face. Her rosy cheeks are covered in moisture now.

"You're always the goody two shoes, thats just who you are, and I love you just the same, Elodie."

I smile sadly, knowing I won't see her for a while and hating it.

"I love you too, Soleil, so so much. You're my sister, no matter what." I take her hands in mine, giving them a squeeze.

Soleil startles me by bursting out into a crying fit. I jump, feeling panic as Fray rushes to her side.

"I didn't, I didn't mean to-" I try, Barre's hands go to my shoulders, I hold onto his fingers for comfort as my best friend continues to openly sob. She covers her face with both hands.

Fray shushes her, guiding her face to his chest as he pets her hair. He prys her fingers away from her eyes. She relents, only to wrap her arms around him, shaking with each sob.

"Do not worry, Elodie. It is not your fault. She is very sensitive. The kit is making her sick with many emotions she is not used to."

Despite his assurance, I bite my lip and want to go to her, comfort her myself as my own cries start to bubble up. I bite my fist, trying to stop myself from reacting the same way. It's not easy. I could very well break down at any moment.

Fray stares at Barre behind me, giving him a look. Since when do they communicate with facial expressions?

My mate turns me around, hands on my shoulders like usual.

"You know, it doesn't have to be this way. You always have a choice." He looks away, not wanting to meet my eyes as he clears his throat.

I feel my eyebrows knit together, my palms starting to become slick with sweat.

"Barre?" I push, and he nods.

"You don't have to be separated, if we stayed here."

"If we stayed... here?"

"Yes, here at the palace. We can live here, if that's what you would want." He relents, his voice quiet and unsure.

He doesn't want that. I don't want that.

"I don't understand. You love your cabin, your pr-property." I stutter, my brain not working properly while his offer sinks in.

This sudden discussion is making my brain go haywire.

Barre's hand goes to my face, and I look deeply into his blue and brown eyes that are so high up it hurts. The look he gives me makes me gasp.

"I do, but I love you more." He says it like it's simple, shrugging his massive, heavy shoulders. "We are partners. It should be a joint decision. We decide these things together."

I never thought I would hear something like that. That speech, that little piece of respect, it's enough to blow me away. This is something I would've never heard if I had been married on Earth. My husband would've kept me under his boot, silent and obedient.

Barre is not a human man, no, he is a Rytarian. A worthy male. A warrior. A gladiator. A partner. An equal.

More tears impossibly bubble up as I think of how sweet he really is.

"I am the luckiest girl on Rytaria." I choke out.

Barre tucks a stray piece of hair from my face as he dabs the salty tears away. His eyes are wide and worried.

"So you want to stay?"

"No, never. I love Soliel, but I want to stay in your den."

"Our den." He corrects me, and I chuckle, nodding my head frantically.

"Yes, our den. I don't know why you would want to stay here, or why you would ever think I would choose this" I motion to the grand castle with a dramatic wave of my arm. "over your cozy cabin. I love it there, it's perfect. It'll be an amazing place to be together, and eventually raise our kits."

I hear a giggle behind me, and I whip around, suddenly defensive.

"What, Soliel? I just poured my heart out, thank you very much." I say, feeling oddly exposed and vulnerable.

I sort of forgot her and Fray were still here.

She holds her stomach, laughing harder.

"Nothing, it's just that you said kits." She slaps a hand to her forehead, taking deep breaths. "Hypocrite."

I press my lips together, trying to hide my amusement.

Fray takes a step forward, lifting a finger in the air and opening his mouth before closing it again. He wants to say something, he;'s just struggling to find the words.

"I was the one who tried to convince Barre it would be better for you to remain in the palace. I now see I was wrong, I'm sorry. It is your decision how best to keep your mate safe." I detect the general remorse in his voice. I still narrow my eyes at him, putting my hands on my hips.

"You didn't think he could keep me safe?" I ask.

Fray is quick to defuse.

"No, no I swear." He tries backpedaling, but Soliel turns on him.

"Did you not see Locanas's face after Barre was done with him? You think he'd let anyone touch her ever again?" Fray shakes his head at his mate, and she nods in satisfaction, looking back to us. "If there was one person on this planet I'd trust to take care of my best friend, it's you Barre. You're the best guy for her."

Barre looks slightly uncomfortable, but also proud and touched by her words. I grin up at him.

"I know so." I murmur, and his eyes are suddenly downcast, reaching his hand out to palm Salsh's head as a distraction from all the unexpected, but very well earned, praise.

A few hugs and tears later, and Barre and I are carrying our own bags through the town.

It was harder leaving Soleil than I thought it would be, but I know that Fray will watch out for her. If not, she's always got her own back, the girl is a spitfire.

Barre and I walk hand in hand to the edge of town. Passersby are watching from the streets and buildings. It's early in the morning, and the scent of fresh baked bread makes my stomach growl in anticipation.

I ignore it all of it. I don't look at a single person as we march proudly. I don't think about the food or small talk to be had. I'm going home. I'm with the love of my life. We're going back to where we belong so we can officially begin our life together.

I don't want to waste a single second. I want to get there as soon as possible.

Finally, after lots of walking, we reach the trees. Barre leads me into the great woods, that's what they call it, and I don't question why it's named that. It's a fitting title. The towering trunks of wood are breathtaking. The canopy of foliage above let's little beams of sunlight through.

As soon as my shoes touch soil, a drop of something hits the tip of my nose. My eyes cross as I try to see what it is, my finger going up to investigate. I pick up the little droplet with the tip of my nail. I inspect it, finding nothing more than a clear fleck of water reflecting the sunlight.

That's when the floodgates really let loose. The sky begins crying on us, dumping rain from above.

I squeal in excitement, not caring at all that my new dress is already soaked and sticking to my skin. A loud rack of thunder shakes the trees. It's a storm of massive proportions, definitely not something soon forgotten. Salsh yips, biting at the raindrops. I laugh, turning to Barre to see him smiling softly down at me.

I grab him by the shirt, pulling him down and standing on the tips of my toes. He has to grab me by the waist and hoist me up to reach my target. I plant my lips on his, letting the rain fuel my desire and passion.

He kisses me back ferociously, claiming my mouth in a hot mix of breath and tug. His big, strong hand holds my neck in place as he has his way with me. His hot tongue delves past my teeth, waring with my own tongue. I start panting, and that's his que to cut it off before we start something we can't stop.

It ends as quick as it began, but Barre doesn't let me down, instead he swings my legs over his arm. He starts walking as if my weight has no effect on his whatsoever. I grin mischievously.

"It would seem the forest is welcoming you back." He muses, kissing my neck and making me shiver with fiery hot intensity. "It gave you what you wanted."

I lean forward, whispering in his ear.

"I can think of something I want more." I nibble his earlobe. "We might have to stop sooner rather than later, because all I can imagine is laying under the trees in the rain with my big, strong male on top of me, filling me with kits."

I try to fake a husky, sexy voice, but end up sounding ridiculous. However, when I pull away and look at Barre's face, his smile has disintegrated.

He starts walking faster, taking a quick glance backwards.

"Whatever my mate wants, she gets."

Chapter 30

Barre

I am eager to get back to my den. The sun cycles spent traveling through the great woods goes by a lot quicker this time around. It's likely due to the fact that I am eager to travel fast, versus before when I did not want to give Elodie up, so I opted to spend as much time as possible with her.

The journey takes a scarce few days, most of it spent carrying my very pretty mate. Her legs are little and weak. Elodie would always have moments where she wanted to walk, saying she is well and able. I would allow it for a while, but always ended up scooping her up into my arms. I didn't have the heart to tell her it was because she was too slow.

As we get closer, Salsh starts to get antsy, and Elodie fights to keep up with the rasler and his never ending energy. I let myself grin. I find it freeing to be able to show my emotions here, because in the palace I had to hide everything I felt, unused to the crowds of males watching me.

Now though, I am able to smile and laugh as much as Elodie permits me.

My mate looks back at me, waving an arm to try to quicken me.

"Come on, Barre! Hurry up, slow poke." She insists, blissfully unaware that I'm walking to match her little human pace.

I allow myself my normal stride. My longer legs, and experience with the forest floor, has me surpassing Elodie much swifter than she had imagined.

"Hey! Wait up." I shake with deep laughter, slowing once more and throwing an arm over her shoulders.

"Make up your mind, tiny."

"I'm not tiny, you're just huge." Elodie insists, folding her arms over her chest as she stumbles over a tree root. "I'm actually considered tall on Earth."

I roll my eyes, not believing her. There is no way that humans come that much smaller than my mate.

Grinning, I realize I don't mind it at all. I like her being small. For one, she relies on me, for another, I can toss her around the nest easily. She also bends all types of ways, ways I never imagined. I find I like our nest play more than I ever thought possible.

I rake my hungry eyes over her. My kit may already be firmly planted in her warm little womb. We mate many times a day.

"Look! There it is!" Elodie's exuberant voice pulls me from my daze. I knew we were close to my home, but thinking of all the naughty things my little human female does with me made me too distracted to realize just how close we really were.

I halt, reaching for my mate's hand and squeezing it as she stops at my side. I look from her smile to the cabin. This is our den. Our future. Our life together. It's everything good that we have ahead of us.

Looking at all the land I own, I no longer see solitude. Instead, I picture little kits running around. I see my mate, rounded belly and orange hair, picking from the vegetable garden and smiling at me as I bring home a fresh kill from the great woods.

"Let's go." She urges, and I can never say no, so I let her lead me wherever she pleases.

Salsh immediately lays down on the front porch, and Eldoie stops to pat him on the head. The cabin is just as we left it, rain drizzling down onto the roof, not another person in sight or even remotely close by. No one will bother us here. It's just me and her.

We're about to walk through the front door when Elodie stops me with a little hand on my chest. Her fingers are nimble and warm, and I can hardly think when they're touching me.

"Wait." Elodie tells me, thoughts warring on her sweet, freckle dotted face. "There's an old fashioned Earth tradition that I want to try. We dont have to do it thought if you think it's stupid."

I hear the vulnerability in her voice. I'm quick to soothe her nerves any time, whatever they may be.

I take her in close to me, pressing her against my middle and loving every bit of it.

"Whatever it is, I'm sure it's not stupid." I press, trying to get her comfortable enough to share her customs with me.

Elodie twiddles her fingers nervously.

"Well, humans, when they get married. Well, married you know, ;ike marriage. Wait, do you guys do that?"

"What is married?"

She gives me a shocked look, sputtering before she can continue explaining.

"Well it's like being mates, so once two people are mated they go on a honeymoon."

"A... honeymoon?" I ask, sounding out the odd word.

"Yeah, a honeymoon! And the man, I mean the male, well he would carry his mate though the threshold of the house to start the honeymoon. That's how they used to do it on Earth a long time ago. I used to read about it all the time, and I always thought it was so romantic, and I always wished it could happen for me."

Thats enough explanation for me. I lift her into me arms,wrapping her legs and arms around me.

"No! Not like that." She tells me, hardly able to speak from the giggling.

I smile, trying something different.

I throw her over my shoulder, her stomach going into my shoulder. My mate's giggling turns into a full blown fit of laughter. I figure I'm doing it right, and I reach for the doorknob, kicking the door open with my boot and stomping into the den.

Stomping into the kitchen, I place Elodie on the counter, putting my hands on either side of her as I lean in for a quick kiss.

I sling both of our bags from my shoulders, looking at my human with a small grin.

"Now our honeymoon can begin." I tell her, noticing how quickly her face turns red.

Elodie looks as if she's trying hard not to laugh as she climbs down off the counter. I put my hands on her hips to help her down. She tries to shew me away, but I ignore her, placing her gently on her feet.

She leans down and starts digging through her bag, she pulls out a little bag of snacks, choosing to put them away in one of the lower cabinets.

"What else do they do on these honeymoons?"

Elodie makes a choking sound and stands up quickly, turning around from the cabinet.

"Ummm. Well people do a lot of things on honeymoons."

"Like what?" I wonder, striding closer to her, hands swinging at my sides.

She begins to act flustered, shutting the cabinet and rummaging through the bag before zipping it up. She doesn't realize I'm right behind her until she turns around. My mate gasps, putting her hand to her chest.

I reach up, brushing her bare arm with her knuckles. Shivers break out across her pale skin. The tiny, red hairs stand on end. Usually these signs would tell me that she's cold, but I know better. I know exactly what I'm doing to her as the fragrance of her arousal spreads through the room. It's intoxicating.

Leaning in close, I press my lips against her ear and murmur words that I know will make her crazy with want.

"You still pretend to be shy when this morning you pounced on me like a hungry rasler." I whisper heatedly. Eldoie's breath catches.

I shuffle closer, pinning her to the wall behind her. My arm goes up to block any way out. She's not getting away from me, not when her need is pounding at me like the thunder that rumbles outside.

"What else do they do on these Earth honeymoons, my sweet tiny?" My voice is now breathy, husky with want and a need so profound that it's hard to breathe correctly.

"You know what." She responds, standing on the tips of her toes and trying to manuaver so that my lips will touch hers.

I straighten, barely out of her reach. I grin slyly.

"Not that easy." I say. "I want to hear you say it."

My teasing has the effect I was looking for. Her skin further flushes. The skin on her chest and all the way up to her neck is aflame with color.

"They mate. Have sex. Make love. They romp around in the sheets over and over, like freaking rabbits. Is that what you wanted me to say?"

I'm not sure what a rabbit is, but the light in her green eyes is enough. I reward her with the kiss shewas wanting earlier.

Our lips collide feverishly, back and forth, push and pull of energy, heat and love. I love this female with everything I am. Everything I have is hers. I am at her mercy. I may be powerful, I may be the strongest thing to roam Rytaria, but she has me right in the palm of her hand.

Her skin is so soft to the touch, like the sweetest fruit. Ripe but just out of reach. Worth all the trouble.

I pull away, loving the way her lips are full and swollen, the way her red eyebrows pull together in aroused confusion caused by my attack.

"May I make love to you?" I ask reverently, kissing each and every one of the knuckles on her right hand.

She gulps, acting as if she needs to think about it for a moment.

Suddenly she nods exuberantly. "Only if you catch me." Before I have a chance to figure out what she means, she ducks under my elbow and darts through the den.

I growl, chasing after her and all that she represents. Always.

Chapter 31

Barre

"Barre!!!"

The sound that Elodie makes is otherworldly. It scrapes against my ears like a weapon of destruction. I rush to the cabin, throwing down my work as if it's wronged me. The animal hide and knife I wield go flying as I flee my hunting shed.

Rain pours around me, lightning lighting the sky with brilliant but dangerous light.

My ears strain as I run up the stairs. I knew I heard her call my name. She was desperate, loud. She needs me. And at a time like this, I can't risk anything.

Slamming the door open, I'm immediately met with Salsh, who proceeds to bark angrily at me. I shove past him, thundering through the house even as real thunder echoes my steps from the storm outside.

"Tiny?" I shout, glancing in the kitchen quickly before moving to the living room but my mate still escapes me. I continue to race until I catch her clutching the sides of the tub.

Her pale, smooth belly sticks out from the water, her face painted with pain.

"The baby.. The baby is coming." She bites out through clenched teeth. My mouth falls open. I don't know what to do for a moment. Its as if time itself has stopped around me, and I'm the only thing that can get it started again.

I push off the doorframe, my body gravitating towards her. Elodie immediately grabs at my hands trying to get me closer. I bend at the knees, lifting her very pregnant body from the bathwater. Her wet skin drips all over me, making my clothes stick to me.

"Barre, it hurts." She moans, clutching her big stomach.

Over the past months spent growing our kit, the doctor has assured me that it is very normal for childbirth to be painful. The reminder of the doctor has me turning to Salsh.

His ears are set upright, fully at attention as he watches me. At his side is a rasler pup I picked up recently, no taller than Salsh's tail. I decided since Elodie became heavy with child that we were in need of more protection when I'm not able to attend to her fully. Salsh has made it his mission to teach the young pup which Elodie has named Freddie. I tried to not react to the odd name.

"Salsh, fetch Doctor Johnston." I command, and he takes off running. Freddie follows closely behind, tripping over himself.

I carry Elodie to our room, slipping her naked body onto the blankets and pushing her face away from her face. Her orange strands stick to her freckle dotted cheeks. She's panting, and her green eyes are dull with agony.

My teeth clench together as she grips my hand with all her little strength will allow her.

"I wish I could take this pain on myself." I insist, shame gripping me as I watch my mate writhe in pain. I watch helplessly as her body tenses up. Her whole stomach hardens like a rock, the skin pulling across her belly as she tries to control her breathing.

"Aggghh."

"I know, I know." I murmur, petting her forehead. I have felt many kinds of pain, but I'm slowly realizing maybe I have not experienced anything like this. "You are a warrior. You are my little warrior."

She nods her head, but doesnt look convinced.

The door swings open, and my desperate eyes fly to the human female in the doorway. It's the doctor.

She's different from the other females I've met, but that is not a bad thing.

"Did her water break?" She barks the question at me, and I shoot her a desperate look at her.

"What?"

She rolls her dark eyes, parting my mate's legs as she puts on a pair of gloves.

"Her amniotic sac, did it break? Is that why she's wet?"

"No, she was taking a bath. I do not know what an amniotic sac is."

She looks inside my mate, nodding her head as she puts her fingers there.

"She's already dilated, I'd say about 7 centimeters."

I glare at her, not liking all of these unfamiliar words she's using around me.

"But that's so soon!" Elodie groans, her stomach tightening once again, she's in so much pain that she can no longer speak through it.

"It seems to be a quick labor. It could be due to the fact that it's an accelerated pregnancy. This baby is ready to come out." Doctor Johnston explains, wiping her arm across her forehead. Her skin is very dark, darker than I've ever seen. Her hair is short but thick and curly.

Elodie gasps for air, gripping my hand tighter as sweat slicks her fingers.

"He's ready to meet his Momma." She tells me, and I watch as she smiles lovingly up at me.

My heart stutters. I bend to kiss her roughly, ending the kiss with a tender peck.

"I'm not convinced its a male just yet. I'm still holding out." I tell her, my heart set on a little red haired female that resembles my mate in both beauty and spirit.

Elodie chuckles despite the agony still displayed all over her.

"This kit is a gladiator, just like his Pa."

A Pa. I am going to be a Pa.

I feel the blood drain from my face, even as my mate tenses once again as Elodie screams.

"You're okay, Dad. You need to be strong for her, okay?" Doctor Johnston's voice barely pierces through my brain fog. I climb off my knees, sitting beside my mate as tears roll down her perfect face.

I pull her onto my lap, determined to hold her against me.

"You're at a 9, Elodie, pretty soon I'm going to ask you to push."

"WHAT? Already?" My female demands, and I know I've never heard her sound so fierce in all the time I've known her. "That can't be right."

"Oh, it's right. Like I said, this baby is ready to be out. Are you ready?"

Elodie shoots me a panicked look, throwing her head back to see me.

"No, no. I don't think I am. I don't think I can do this."

I can see that Doctor Johnston is trying not to smile with amusement. I feel a spark of anger, but turn to my mate instead.

She needs me to be strong for her. For us. We are a family. I see the unsurety in her gaze, hear the trembling in her voice. I grab her face, leaning until her eyes meet mine. She's afraid. I despise that fear, but understand it. I cannot begin to fathom the pain she is experiencing.

"Tiny. You can do this. You do not admit defeat." I insist, my voice gruff. "I do not need to tell you how strong you are, because you already know."

Even though her lip trembles, even though her little body shakes, she fixes her jaw and nods her head up at me.

"Good girl." I praise, and her eyes twinkle as she refaces the female Doctor.

"You're a 10. You can start pushing."

Push she does. Baring her weight down on me, her whole body is tense as she screams with her effort. My mouth drops open witnessing it.

Elodie pushes, and pushes again, and again. Her power knows no limits as she refuses to be defeated by delivering our kit. Even Doctor Johnston's eyes widen as my mate battles in the bed for her victory.

"Here it comes! You're doing it, Elodie!" She encourages, and Elodie uses that momentum to finish it.

With a few more pushes, a newborn cry breaks the air. Elodie collapses in my lap, panting and gasping for air as exhaustion already makes her lids start drooping.

Our kit continues crying, and I'm hungry for a look at it. The Doctor quickly severs the tie between mother and child, bringing our baby to place in Elodie's shaking arms.

"Mother's intuition. There's something to be said about that." She winks, slipping the little bundle down to us. "It's a boy. Congratulations."

Elodie gasps, parting the blanket so we can take a look at our son.

His face is scrunched and angry, little fists swinging. His hair is dark like mine. The hair is plastered to his head. He's covered in blood and a white film. He's fresh from his mother's warm womb, and he's not too thrilled about it.

"My son." I murmur, cupping the side of the struggling bundle as tears fill my eyes. "Our son."

Elodie giggles, though she is crying too. She caressed his little, chubby cheeks with her fingertips, her hands still quivering from the ordeal.

And what an ordeal it was. I can scarcely believe we made it out the other side.

I pull my mate close to me, still snuggled in my lap, our kit going quiet in her arms as he blinks up at us. His eyes are light blue, like all babies, but I hope and pray to the gods that those shimering eyes will turn green like Eldoei's.

"We did good, Barre. Look at him." I look away from our child, focusing on her face above all else.

"You did good, my sweet mate. You fought and did not admit defeat." I grab her hand tightly and pulling it to my mouth, kissing each knuckle.

She beams at the praise, straining forward for a kiss. I grant it, before tucking her head into my neck and admiring my family over and over again.

Salsh and Freddie burst in the room, running past Doctor Johnston and jumping onto the nest. They sniff curiously at our son, but quickly lay at the end of the covers to stand guard. I smile at their nature.

Not so long ago I had nothing. I was alone. Desolate. A monster hidden in the shadows. I had no idea what was to come, the blessing that the gods would grant me. It all started on that fateful day, the day I found Elodie in the woods, hurt and alone. I may have saved her that day, but in reality, she was the one that saved me.

"My Elodie, my sweet tiny mate, I did not live until I met you." I whisper to her, watching more tears flood her face as she nods.

"Me neither, Barre. This is the life I've always dreamed of. I love you."

I couldn't have said it better myself.

CPSIA information can be obtained
at www.ICGtesting.com
Printed in the USA
LVHW040241020323
740706LV00017B/1481

9 781944 115135